Books should be returned or renewed by the
last date stamped above.

Lennox, Joanne
Heart of deception

HEART OF DECEPTION

HEART OF DECEPTION

Joanne Lennox

CHIVERS
THORNDIKE

This Large Print book is published by BBC Audiobooks Ltd, Bath, England and by Thorndike Press®, Waterville, Maine, USA.

Published in 2006 in the U.K. by arrangement with the author.

Published in 2006 in the U.S. by arrangement with Joanne Lennox.

U.K. Hardcover ISBN 1–4056–3668–8 (Chivers Large Print)
U.K. Softcover   ISBN 1–4056–3690–4 (Camden Large Print)
U.S. Softcover   ISBN 0–7862–8494–3 (British Favorites)

The text of this Large Print edition is unabridged.
Other aspects of the book may vary from the original edition.

Set in 16 pt. New Times Roman.

Printed in Great Britain on acid-free paper.

British Library Cataloguing in Publication Data available

Library of Congress Cataloging-in-Publication Data

Lennox, Joanne.
      Heart of deception / by Joanne Lennox.
        p.   cm.
     "Thorndike Press large print British favorites."—T.p. verso.
     ISBN 0–7862–8494–3 (lg. print : sc : alk. paper)
     I. Title.
PR6062.E647H43 2006
823'.92—dc22   2006005679

CHAPTER ONE

'I'm just off for an early lunch, then,' Susie, the young shop assistant, called brightly, clearly eager to escape.

Lily Mason glanced up, in the process of tying her overall.

'OK. See you later, Susie.' She smiled. The bell jingled as the door slammed shut. Lily's smile faded as her thoughts reclaimed her.

Moments later, the bell of the little corner shop jingled again, causing Lily to be jolted out of her brooding, troubled reverie. The door swung closed as a tall, brown-haired man strode into the shop. A customer, Lily reminded herself. She couldn't shirk her duties, even though there were too many worries on her mind, and she wasn't really in the mood. She owed it to Dad to carry on as normal. Facing the man, she tossed back her blonde ponytail, and pinned her best smile to her face. 'Can I help you?'

The man stared at her.

Rude, Lily thought, as her smile stretched to breaking point.

'I haven't seen you here before, have I?' the man asked her, in a low, quizzical tone, his head cocked to one side.

'Maybe not,' Lily replied tightly, determined to give away as little as possible.

1

'Are you the new girl, then?' he probed, a golden glint in his tawny brown eyes.

So he was not only rude, but nosy, too.

'I haven't been working here that long, if that's what you mean. Now,' Lily asked as politely as she could, 'how can I help you, sir?'

'Oh, well, I'd like a bottle of your finest champagne, please,' the man said casually. Lily glanced at him, taken aback. She wasn't sure, at first, if his tongue was in his cheek. In fact, a few weeks ago even she would have doubted whether her father's corner shop stocked such a thing as champagne.

The man was gazing expectantly at her, with those tawny eyes—he certainly didn't look as if he was joking.

'Certainly,' Lily replied, going to the small refrigerator that stood against one wall. Opening it, she took out a bottle of Bollinger. Returning to the counter, she rolled the cold bottle in a sheet of blue paper.

'That will be seventeen pounds, please.'

'A bargain.' The man grinned back.

As she outstretched her hand for the man's money, Lily remembered what her dad, poor, dear Dad, had said to her, blue eyes crinkling at the corners. 'The customers love a bit of small talk, Lil. Gives them a personal connection to the place.'

Lily cleared her throat now.

'So,' she asked, with a sunny smile, as the man flipped open his wallet, 'got something to celebrate, have you?' With mock-primness she added, 'At this hour on a Saturday lunchtime?'

The man glanced up at her. A hank of brown hair had flopped across his eyes and Lily silently caught her breath, suddenly realising how attractive he was. Impatiently, the man pushed the hank of hair away.

'You could say that,' he replied with a sudden, slow grin. 'My decree absolute arrived in the post today. My divorce has finally come through.'

'Oh!' Lily exclaimed, her blue eyes surprised. Her cheeks flushed slightly. 'I would have thought the end of a marriage was more a cause for commiseration.' She bit her lip, fearing she had been too rude.

The man shrugged and said, 'Celebration, commiseration, whatever. It's time to move on. And I might as well do it in style. Here.' He offered her a slightly crumpled twenty pound note.

Lily took the note, her blood suddenly cooling as she remembered the events of two days ago. She smoothed the note out between her hands, before holding it up to the meagre light from the shop window.

She heard her father's voice saying, 'Check the thread, check the watermark. We've had too many of these fakes lately, and we simply can't afford it.'

Lily lowered the note. Everything appeared to be in order.

3

'What's the matter?' the man raised one eyebrow at her now. 'Think I'm trying to slip you a dodgy note?'

'You can't be too careful,' she replied, as the till drawer slid obediently open, with a ching. 'We've had a spate of fake ones lately.'

About to slip the note safely inside, Lily's hand froze. She slid her fingers over the surface on the top note in the pile in the till, then, with a shaky hand, she slowly swapped it for the one she held in her hand.

Her heart like lead, Lily studied the other note from the till. Instinctively she knew that something was wrong. It didn't feel right—too smooth, soapy smooth. And the watermark was visible even without light.

'What's the matter?' the man asked from the other side of the counter, sounding concerned now.

'Oh, no!' Lily muttered, tears prickling her eyes. She thrust the note angrily away from her. 'Another fake.' She leaned heavily on the counter with both hands, as if for strength. 'That's half today's profit down the drain already,' she muttered, half to herself. 'I can't believe it.'

'Hey, that's bad luck,' the man replied. 'I'm sorry.'

'It certainly is,' Lily replied feelingly. Her fists tightened. 'I'd love to get my hands on the creeps who distribute these things. Oh, well,' she sighed. Putting the fake note to one side, Lily made herself return to business. She counted out the man's change, handing it to him. 'Anyway, it's OK,' she forced herself to say. 'You don't have to apologise. It's not your fault.'

About to take his champagne and go, the man hesitated.

'So, you get a lot of fake notes in here, then?' When she did not immediately reply he added, 'Is this an ongoing situation, can I ask, or has there been a sudden increase lately?'

Lily sighed exasperatedly, and said, 'You certainly ask a lot of questions, don't you?' she burst out. 'And anyway,' she went on, her blue eyes looking challengingly at him from beneath the white-blonde fringe, 'I've only been working here for a couple of weeks.'

'Of course, you did mention that.' He looked at her curiously again. 'Please, do accept my apologies for my nosiness.' The man shifted his bottle of champagne to the crook of his left arm, extending his right hand to her. 'Tom McCleod,' he introduced himself. 'And I'm sorry if I seem overly inquisitive, but the subject of counterfeit money is one that particularly interests me.'

Lily didn't have the chance to ask him why, because at that moment the shop bell jingled again and a man came in dressed in workmen's clothes, bought a newspaper and a chocolate bar and left.

Lily wished the other man in her shop was

5

as easy to get rid of.

'Was there something else you wanted, Mr McCleod?' she asked the tall, good-looking man, who was still casually regarding her, as if sizing her up, or trying to place her.

Tom McCleod came forward to the counter, and set his bottle of champagne back down again.

'Yes, there was, actually,' he said, his tone having taken on a sudden urgency, as if he realised their time to talk was brief. He met her eyes with new frankness. 'I'm a senior reporter for the Brighton Clarion. I'd really like to do an article on all the counterfeit money that's currently flying around in the area. Would you let me interview you, um . . .' His tawny-brown eyes looked expectantly at her, for her name.

'Lily,' she supplied reluctantly, deeming that he did not need to know her surname. 'So that explains your natural inquisitiveness,' Lily concluded with wry cynicism. 'You're a journalist.' It fitted, she thought, looking covertly at him from beneath her dark lashes.

The bell jingled once again, heralding another customer.

'So, what do you say, Lily?' Tom McCleod demanded of her urgently, under his breath, as a lanky teenage boy went over to the shelf to select a packet of crisps. 'Will you give me an interview?'

'I don't know,' Lily replied. She enjoyed her

6

own privacy, and had an inbuilt wariness of the Press, of people like Tom McCleod, not to mention men in general, since what had happened between her and Ryan.

'You said yourself you wanted to take action against the people who do things like this,' Tom reminded her in a low voice, his brown hair flopping into his eyes again. He pushed the hair aside. 'This is your chance to expose the scourge of counterfeiting, and help other small businesses like the one you work for.'

The teenager came over to pay for his crisps and magazine.

'I'll have to think about it,' Lily told Tom, instinctively shying away from his pushiness. Tom was scribbling on a scrap of paper on the top of the counter. The boy, meanwhile, took his purchases and left.

'Here's my number,' Tom said, thrusting the piece of paper at her.

'Enjoy your champagne,' Lily called across the shop as an impulsive afterthought, and was rewarded by a lazy grin.

*   *   *

'Well, sweetheart, did you have a good day?'

'Hmm.' Coming into the small sitting-room of the flat above the shop, Lily hesitated. 'Well, yes and no. Yes, in that trade was quite brisk . . .'

7

'And no in that . . .' Her father prompted, his blue eyes looking shrewdly at her.

Lily dreaded telling her father that she had found the second fake note of the week in the till that lunchtime.

'Promise me you won't be shocked, Dad,' she urged.

Edward Mason wasn't supposed to have shocks, not since his mild heart attack three weeks ago, well, the doctors had called it mild but it had certainly shaken up Lily and her father, at the time.

She told him about the fake note. He shook his fair head sadly.

'I told you how to check the notes, love,' he said, with a faint hint of reproach.

Lily sat bolt upright on the sofa, indignant.

'I did, Dad!' she burst out, without thinking. 'I swear!'

'Ah.' Her father nodded slowly, in sudden comprehension. He sighed. 'So it was young Susie again, was it?'

Instantly, Lily felt guilty that she had implicated the teenager.

'It wasn't Susie's fault, Dad,' she said, leaping to the girl's defence. 'She's only seventeen, and she's very reliable, most of the time. And I had a careful chat with her afterwards,' Lily added.

'I'm sure you did, love,' Edward, or Eddie, as he was known to his male friends in the community, assured her. He leaned back on

8

the armchair cushions. 'And I don't mean to blame you, or Susie.' He sighed heavily, his anxious eyes gazing unseeingly at the television screen. 'It's just that the business is struggling as it is, and something like this could really push us under. I just feel so, so powerless to fight it.'

A week and a half later, on the Tuesday evening, Lily carried that week's copy of the Brighton Clarion into the flat's narrow hallway with her after work. She had already glanced at the banner headline, COUNTERFEIT CASH THREAT TO LOCAL BUSINESSES and noticed, underneath, Tom McCleod's byline.

In the middle of a crowded shop, her heart had leaped in recognition. Now, Lily carried the paper slowly upstairs, already absorbed in reading the article, which covered much of the front page. There was even a small, blurry photograph of herself, she noticed with embarrassment, holding up a fake note and looking indignant. Tom himself had taken the picture outside her father's shop, after he'd interviewed her.

'It's only me, Dad!' she called now. 'I'm back.'

'Hiya, love,' her father's voice called back from the sitting-room.

Without taking her eyes off the newspaper, Lily negotiated a doorway, sank on to a chair at the kitchen table, kicked off her shoes, and continued to read Tom McCleod's report.

Tom hadn't seemed surprised when she'd rung his number, on the evening of that same Saturday they'd met. The following Sunday, during Lily's lunch-break from the shop, they'd met up in the café round the corner, which both had judged to be neutral ground.

'Let's sit here,' Tom had said, steering her towards a secluded table at the back of the small, Italian café.

'So,' Tom switched his small, portable cassette recorder on, 'What's your full name?' When she told him, he twigged that she was the daughter of Edward Mason, the man who owned Mason's corner shop. 'So you really have got a vested interest in tackling this counterfeiting business,' he commented.

Lily nodded feelingly.

'How is Eddie, by the way?' Tom asked, pausing the cassette recorder. 'I haven't seen him in the shop lately.' And so, before she told him of her experiences with counterfeit money, Lily had to tell Tom McCleod the traumatic saga of her father's heart attack, and her temporarily leaving her well-paid job as a database administrator, to come and help him out.

Now, over a week later, reading Tom's finished article in the comfort of her father's kitchen, Lily had to admire his skill in putting together such a polished article, based on the snippets of information she'd given him. She

10

was just pushing the Brighton Clarion to one side, and wondering whether to make a cup of coffee to take into her father, in the sitting-room, when the phone rang. Lily's spirits rose slightly. Maybe it would be her best friend, Jenny, ringing to say she'd seen her on the front page of the paper.

'It's all right, Dad,' she called, going across the kitchen to answer the phone. 'I'll get it. Hello?' she said into the receiver.

'Lily,' the voice at the other end said. 'It's me, Tom.'

'Oh,' Lily replied. 'Hello.'

'Don't sound so disappointed,' Tom said wryly. There was a pause. He added casually, 'Seen the article yet?'

'I've just read it.' Lily leaned against the worktop. 'It's very good,' she admitted grudgingly, annoyed by the calm confidence in Tom's tone.

'Glad you think so,' Tom replied with a half-laugh. 'You're not the only one, either,' he went on. 'We've already had some very positive feedback about it from members of the public. Colin, my editor, seems pretty chuffed with it, too.'

'Well, I'm glad I was of assistance in furthering your career, Tom,' she said, dry amusement in her tone. 'Maybe I'll see you in the shop sometime in the future, next time you want a bottle of champagne. Goodbye then . . .'

11

'Wait a minute,' Tom interrupted firmly. 'Don't hang up. I haven't got to the real reason for my call yet. It wasn't purely a social one. You see . . .'

'Ye-es?' Lily asked, suddenly wary, and wishing she had a chair nearby to sink down on to.

'Well,' Tom's casual tones went on, 'because Colin, my editor, liked the article so much, and because it went down so well, he wants more.'

'More?' Lily asked, bemused.

'More,' Tom agreed. 'The thing is, with Colin pestering me constantly, I've been thinking about how we could investigate this counterfeit cash thing further, and I've come up with an idea.'

'I was afraid you were going to say that,' Lily said wearily.

'Hey! You said you'd love to get your hands on the creeps putting this dodgy money about, didn't you?' Tom asked. 'Well, I've thought of a way in which we could try and infiltrate their criminal world. You see, I've got a few contacts of my own, and . . .'

'Their criminal world?' Lily echoed, her hand feeling suddenly clammy on the telephone receiver. 'Somehow I don't like the sound of that.'

'You don't have to get involved if you don't want to,' Tom assured her, down the line, 'but I promise I'll do my best to keep you safe.

Now, if you do agree to come in on this with me,' he went on, 'I'll pick you up tomorrow evening, at nine, in my car.'

'Sounds innocuous enough, I suppose,' Lily replied.

'So you're in, then?' Tom asked. 'Excellent.' As if about to hang up, he added, 'Oh, and there's just one more thing.'

'What's that?' Lily asked, feeling more relaxed now.

'For tomorrow, I'm going to try and hang out around the city's pubs and pose as a member of the criminal underworld. So, needless to say,' he went on, delivering his bombshell, 'I'll require you to be dressed up as my girlfriend.'

CHAPTER TWO

Lily didn't like to think too closely about what exactly Tom McCleod had in mind for their night of investigative journalism together. Nor did she like to think too much about why she was placing so much trust in a man she had barely met.

Just before nine, with the sky darkening outside her bedroom window, the doorbell rang. Glancing down through the pane, Lily saw a sporty red car parked in the road outside, which she presumed must be Tom's. The doorbell rang again, more impatiently this time.

'OK, OK, I'm coming!' she called, as Tom pressed the doorbell for a third time.

'D'you want me to let your friend in, Lil?' her father called from across the hallway.

'No!' Lily cried, adding, 'No, thanks, Dad! Anyway, I'm off out now, see you later.' She almost broke her neck rushing down the stairs in her tight skirt and heels to get to the door.

'Wow!' Tom drawled, staring at her as she opened the front door. It was a couple of moments before he managed to speak again. 'If I'd met you in the street, Lily, I'm not sure I would have known it was the same woman.'

They stepped outside into the evening air.

'I have to say, you look stunning, Lily,' Tom

told her, as he zapped the key-fob to unlock the car doors.

'Another compliment?' Lily asked in surprise, seating herself in the sun-warmed car. She had thought Tom was too cool a customer for that.

'I know. I don't normally believe in lavishing women with compliments,' he teased, getting into the driver's seat. 'It makes them big-headed. It's just that, well, you've blown me away tonight,' he went on, his tone suddenly serious. Again, to her annoyance, Lily blushed. So he'd thought she was some frumpy little shop girl, did he?

'So,' she asked, changing the subject to something safer, 'where are we off to?'

She glanced across at Tom as he concentrated on the road ahead. He was looking good, too, she had to admit, in stylish, expensive-looking jeans and a blue shirt, blatantly displaying its designer logo.

'First, we're heading slightly out of town.' He flicked her a quick look. 'We're taking a trip to Sainsbury's.'

At the wine and spirits aisle Tom finally parked the trolley.

'What the heck are you doing?' Lily demanded under her breath, as Tom picked up two bottles of liqueur, one in each hand, and placed them carefully in the trolley.

'Don't you worry, Lil, just leave me to get on with it. I'll explain once we've paid.'

15

Tom selected bottles of brandy, and then two of whisky, gin and vodka. He paid the astronomic bill for the alcohol without batting an eyelid, tucking the receipt into his wallet.

Then, when they were driving back towards the city centre, the box clanking away in the boot, Tom suddenly said, in a low, serious voice, 'You see, Lily, what we're going to do is to use that alcohol as our passport into Brighton's criminal underworld.'

They parked in a carpark on the sea front, at the end of a long street where several of Brighton's busiest pubs were located.

Lily frowned at him in the street light.

'Aren't you worried about leaving your swanky car in a place like this at this time of night, Tom?'

'Not really,' Tom replied, shifting the heavy box a bit higher. 'It's got an alarm, and an engine immobiliser. It should be OK. Come on,' he added.

Feeling vulnerable and under-dressed, Lily did as he bade her.

'Let's try the Three Horseshoes first,' Tom suggested, as they approached a large, traditional-looking pub. Lily felt more bemused than ever, and suddenly felt desperate to know what was going on.

She turned to her companion, her eyes full of an urgent appeal.

'So what is it you're hoping to do then, Tom?' she demanded, under her breath.

16

Tom grinned at her across the top of the box, his tawny brown eyes glinting in the streetlight and said, 'Just watch, Lily, and you'll see.'

Tom negotiated his way through the throng to the bar, Lily close on his heels. He dumped his box unceremoniously on the top of the bar, with a thud and a clank of bottles. Immediately Tom's actions caught the attention of the landlord, who hurried over to them.

Tom leaned across the bar to speak to the balding, middle-aged man. Lily leaned forward, too, only just catching his voice above the noise of the other pub customers.

'You, uh, interested in buying some dodgy booze?' Tom asked.

There was a split second's pause and then, 'No,' the publican replied quickly and firmly. He looked anxiously around him before adding sharply, 'Now get that stuff out of here, before I call the police.'

'But, Tom, that booze isn't dodgy!' Lily protested, baffled, as they emerged from the smoky fug of the pub, into the fresh night air.

'I know,' Tom replied, slightly out of breath from the strain of lugging the box. 'But we've got to pretend it is,' he hissed. 'Dodgy booze is the only sort of booze the criminal world will be interested in.'

They tried two more pubs in the same street after that, the Prince Regent and the

White Hart, only to be turned away on both occasions. Lily trailed wearily after Tom's tall figure into the Beachcomber, suspecting that they would find the same response there, too.

'You interested in buying some dodgy booze?' Tom asked the man behind the bar.

'You want Gerry,' the man replied. 'Hang on a mo'.'

Liz shivered, despite the warmth of the pub, suddenly full of foreboding.

'Tom,' she murmured under her breath. 'Let's go now. I don't like this one little bit . . .'

'You wanted to speak to me?' A man, who was presumably Gerry, had appeared in the doorway behind the bar. He was in his mid-fifties, Lily guessed, looking across at him, stockily built with dyed black hair.

The man came closer to them, smiling briefly, a smile that didn't reach his eyes. They were of a cold, calculating grey-blue, and Lily noted that they didn't go naturally with the hair.

'What's this about dodgy booze?' Gerry added under his breath, as if loathe to be overheard by his bustling crowd of pub clientele.

Tom gestured towards the crate shrugging nonchalantly and said, 'Take a look, if you're interested.'

While Lily's trepidation grew, Gerry glanced at the box full of bottles. There was a brief moment of hesitation, as the middle-

18

aged man looked up at Tom with something approaching suspicion.

'Come through to the back,' Gerry growled suddenly to Tom.

Poised to leave, Gerry's gaze fell on Lily for the first time. The man stared at her. Lily squirmed under his scrutiny, his gaze somehow making her feel cheapened. Then he said, 'Who's this?'

'Oh.' Tom laid a hand on Lily's shoulder. Not for the first time, she felt intensely aware of their point of physical contact. 'This is Jilly, my girl.'

Lily felt her cheeks flame. Her fists clenched involuntarily behind her back, and she struggled to suppress her indignation, both at being rechristened Jilly, and at being presented as Tom's girl. How dare he!

With an effort she reminded herself of what they were setting out to do here, and that she had a part to play.

'Pleased to meet you,' Lily chirruped. She outstretched a slender hand towards the man. 'Nice place you've got here.'

'Very nice,' Gerry commented drily, clasping her fingers and looking at Lily. He released the hand.

With the men gone, a furious Lily retreated to a secluded table for one, to nurse a drink. She glanced at the clock on the pub wall. It was now nearly half-past ten and she had been up since six. To take her mind off the crazy situation she found herself in, Lily had a sip of the drink.

Ten minutes after he had disappeared, and just as Lily was fending off the attentions of a rather the worse-for-wear young man, Tom returned, minus the box of bottles.

'Do I take it your mission was successful, then?' Lily asked in surprise, as Tom pulled up a chair at her table.

'You assume correctly,' Tom muttered under his breath, leaning forward.

Under the table, he showed Lily a wodge of bank notes.

'Phew,' Lily exhaled slowly, impressed, glancing at the notes. 'Not bad.'

'Hmm.' Under the table, Tom fanned out the notes, flicking them one by one past his thumb. 'Maybe not as impressive as it seems, though.'

'What do you mean?' Lily frowned, gazing as the purpley-blue twenties flashed past her eyes.

'I mean,' Tom muttered, 'that I've a strong suspicion these notes aren't all that they appear to be.'

'Fakes, you mean.' Lily felt a now-familiar tingling of foreboding.

Tom shoved the notes back into his pocket, and pushed back his chair, getting to his feet.

'Let's find out for sure.' He picked up Lily's empty glass. 'Same again?'

Lily grabbed the twenty-pound note that

20

was already in his hand.

'Well, maybe you could stay behind and save the table then,' she said and took the empty glass from his other hand. 'I'll get the drinks.'

Tom's normally laidback face looked as if it was struggling to suppress anger.

'Have it your way, then,' he muttered eventually, turning to go back to the table. 'But take care.'

Lily pushed her way through the crowds to the bar. Samantha, the pretty, brunette barmaid, materialised to serve her, her round face wreathed in smiles.

'Same again, love?'

Before Lily had a chance to answer, the barmaid had taken her glass and was pressing it against the optic. 'Anything else?'

'A pint of lager,' Lily said.

'That'll be five pounds, twenty-five, please.'

Suddenly feeling sick with nerves now that the time had come, Lily proffered the twenty-pound note. The barmaid took it, frowned, and held it up to the light.

'Sorry,' she said finally, returning the note to Lily, looking her over with appraising, suspicious brown eyes. 'I can't take that one. It's a fake.'

Lily's heart sank in dismay.

But it was given to us by the publican of this very pub, she wanted to say. Not for the first time that night, however, she bit her lip. She

21

was starting to realise that she was no good at this undercover lark—it didn't come naturally to her to pretend to be something she wasn't.

'OK,' Lily sighed, reaching inside her little, sequinned handbag. From her purse, she extracted a genuine twenty-pound note, offering it to the barmaid. 'Here.'

Lily returned to the table with the drinks.

'Well?' Tom demanded, looking as if he could scarcely contain his impatience.

Lily shook her head, her dismay evident on her face.

'I'm sorry, Tom, but your suspicions were correct.'

She put the drinks down on the table, and sat down wearily.

'Thought as much.' Tom nodded slowly, not looking as upset as she had feared. 'Well, it seems we're definitely on to something here then.'

'Never mind that,' Lily replied in a quiet, anxious voice, 'what are you going to do, Tom? You spent all the money on bottles of spirits, and you've been paid for them in fake notes.'

'That's about the size of it.' Tom nodded at her, grinning wryly.

'Ah,' Lily murmured, in realisation. 'Don't tell me! That was exactly the situation you wanted to engineer, all along.'

'You got it,' Tom confirmed. Lily shook her head in bemused disbelief.

Then, suddenly, it was as if a shadow passed across Tom's face, and the light-hearted mood dispersed again. He set down his pint abruptly, the glass still half-full, and got to his feet.

'Time we were going, I think, sweetheart.' Tom laid a brief hand on Lily's shoulder.

'Don't call me sweetheart,' Lily replied indignantly, shaking off the hand.

Tom bent down, so that his face was closer to hers.

'You're my girlfriend, remember?' he said into her ear, so close that she could smell his aftershave. 'And we're being watched. Our friend, Gerry, is behind the bar now, and he's looking at us suspiciously. So's that barmaid.'

'Oh, I see.' Lily didn't need any second asking. Glancing towards the bar, she saw that they were, indeed, being watched. Lily didn't protest as Tom slipped his arm around her waist, and they made their way out through the pub's main entrance.

Out in the darkness of Prince Regent Street once again, Lily gratefully inhaled the fresh night air.

'So where did Gerry take you, then?' she asked Tom, pulling away from his arm. The pub sign creaked balefully above their heads.

'To a private room, out the back. There were a couple of other unsavoury looking characters in there, too.'

Lily shivered again.

'Like I said before, I don't like this, Tom. I only said I'd get involved to help small businesses like my dad's . . .'

'Yes,' Tom replied, turning to her, a light of eagerness in his eyes. 'And the only way we'll help such small businesses is by getting to the bottom of all this.'

'But where is all this leading, anyway?' Lily asked anxiously.

'Well, in the long term, I'm going to go away, use my contacts, and do some homework on my mate, Gerry, and the charming hostelry known as the Beachcomber.'

'And in the short term?' Lily asked, not really wanting to know.

Tom took her arm, pulling her with him round the gloomy alleyway between the pub and its neighbour, the gaudily-lit Atlantis Casino.

'I'd like to have a bit more of a snoop around here, see if we can discover any more clues about what's going on.'

'Clues?' Lily's heart started to pound with anxiety.

They came to a small, shabby garden at the rear, with a couple of ramshackle pub tables. Suddenly there was the sound of a door slamming from somewhere at the back of the pub and then men's voices, raised in animated discussion.

'Quick, round here.' Tom pulled Lily back round to the alley at the side of the pub, just as Gerry and another man appeared, looking suspiciously around them. Gerry's head appeared round the corner, peering down the alley. Tom and Lily shrank back in the darkness.

'He's seen us.' Lily's voice was no more than a dismayed whisper.

'Come on,' Tom muttered. 'We're a courting couple, remember?'

Quickly he pulled her to him, kissing her with a convincing show of passion. Lily's murmurs of indignance were quickly stifled. To her annoyance she realised that the experience of being kissed by this man was not unpleasant.

'Oi, you two!' Gerry called sharply, his voice echoing down the alleyway. 'Scram!'

Doing her best to look startled, Lily pulled away hastily from Tom's embrace. She smoothed down her hair and allowed Tom to tow her away after him, in an undignified retreat.

Five minutes later, Brighton's night traffic droned on the roads around them.

'We're getting involved with the big boys here. You don't mess around with people like Gerry and his cronies.' She voiced the suspicion that had been troubling her for some time. 'I mean, Gerry's a gangster, isn't he?'

Tom straightened and said, 'I would say that was a pretty fair assumption, yes.'

'And you still haven't really told me what you intend to do next, to pursue your precious investigation,' Lily persisted. 'I'm not really sure I want to be involved in all this any more.'

'Hmm.' Tom frowned, scratching his lightly-stubbled chin, apparently deep in thought. 'Maybe you're right, Lily. Maybe it's time to try a different tack. And I think,' he added mysteriously, 'that Jamie could be just the bloke to help us do it.'

'Jamie?' Lily queried sharply.

Tom nodded and said, 'An old mate of mine. I'll have to introduce the two of you.' He chuckled. 'You'll probably get along like a house on fire.'

CHAPTER THREE

'Meet my mate, Jamie Latham.' Lily gazed first at Tom, and then at the man standing beside him on her doorstep. He was tall with light blue eyes and cropped black hair, shaved close at the back and sides. 'Jamie's an actor,' Tom was going on. 'That's why I thought he might be able to help us.'

As Lily stared at Jamie, mesmerised by his good looks, their eyes locked. Something indefinable passed between them.

Tom seemed to frown at the pair of them.

'Jamie, this is Lily Mason,' he said, completing the introductions.

'Actually,' Jamie Latham said, outstretching a hand, 'I'm currently an out-of-work actor, a resting actor, I believe they say. Anyway, I'm very pleased to meet you, Lily,' he added charmingly.

'Likewise,' Lily replied, regaining her composure enough to take Jamie's large paw of a hand. His grip was predictably warm, firm and muscular. Quickly changing the subject, Lily pointed towards the gleaming, metallic-green Range Rover that stood parked in the road outside her dad's flat.

'What's this, Tom? A new set of wheels? That must have cost you a few bob.'

'Shame it's not mine, though. It belongs to

27

the boss, my editor, Colin,' he elucidated. 'I managed to persuade him to lend it to us.'

'I needed something convincing to drive, you see,' Jamie put in, grinning.

'You'd better take good care of it though, mate.' Tom gave his friend a sidelong look. 'Forget Gerry Lambert. Colin says his wife will be furious if anything happens to the car.' Tom turned back towards Lily. 'What do you think, then, Lil? What's your opinion of my latest plan?'

Glancing at Jamie in the evening sunlight and long shadows, while cars droned past her doorstep, Lily nodded slowly.

'Well, if we're talking about infiltrating criminal gangs,' she said thoughtfully, 'I must admit that Jamie certainly looks more the part than we do.'

Lily looked from Tom towards Jamie, aware that the latter exuded a certain charisma, essential if one wanted to be an actor? Lily cleared her throat, glancing at the hallway behind her.

'Well, I would ask you in, chaps, but . . . well, my father might start asking some interesting questions.'

'Good point,' Jamie agreed.

'Anyway,' Tom said, 'we must get going. Or, more to the point, Jamie must.'

Lily was struck that, contrary to appearances, Tom was far more go-getting than his friend. Despite the crucial rôle that

Jamie had to play, it was Tom who was masterminding the operation.

'Now,' Tom instructed his friend, 'the box of booze is in the boot of the car. Different booze from the other day, of course. All vodka, this time. And if anyone asks, Jamie, it was nicked from a warehouse.' Lily followed the two men across the shadowy pavement to the Range Rover. Tom spoke in an urgent mutter to Jamie. 'Take the box to the Beachcomber pub in Prince Regent Street.'

'Whom do I ask for?' Jamie queried, black eyebrows furrowed.

Tom zapped the keyring at the car. 'Ask for Gerry.'

'What about us?' Lily asked Tom. 'Where are we going?'

'Jamie can drop us off,' Tom replied, holding the car door open for her. 'We've got time to kill, but I don't think the two of us can risk setting foot inside the Beachcomber again in the near future, Lily.'

'No, they seemed suspicious enough last time,' Lily agreed. 'Gerry, and that barmaid. They probably thought we were undercover police.'

Tom nodded, his sun-streaked brown hair flopping into his eyes. He pushed it aside impatiently.

'So, we're agreed that we can't go back to the Beachcomber. And you've said that your home is off-limits, Lily. I suspect you'd read

29

me the riot act if I suggested going back to my place, however innocent my motives,' he added with a wry twist of the mouth, as, inside the Range Rover, they all fastened their seatbelts.

Jamie revved up the car.

'Nice motor,' he yelled appreciatively above the roar of the engine. 'Just getting into character,' he growled, winking at Lily. 'Jimmy Donovan's the name. Wheeler, dealer and friend of the gangsters.'

'So anyway, Tom,' Lily interrupted impatiently, as the Range Rover leaped into life, 'never mind the wear and tear on your boss's engine. You still haven't told me where you're taking me.'

'Well, I thought we might go to a different pub tonight, Ms Mason,' Tom replied, with a careless shrug, 'where we can indulge in pina coladas and some civilised conversation, while we wait for Jamie to report back to us.'

*   *   *

Jamie had dropped them off at the White Hart, a pub farther down Prince Regent Street, before he zoomed off on his way to the Beachcomber.

The pub was busy with Friday crowds, and Lily was lucky to get a table.

'I feel like a mother waiting for her child to come back from its first day at school,' she admitted, as Tom returned from the bar, handing her a white wine spritzer. She sipped the drink, thankful that Tom had been joking about the pina coladas. 'I feel sort of helpless.'

Straddling a stool, Tom said, 'I hate to break the habit of a lifetime, but for once I'm in agreement with you, Lily. It's not really my style to stand on the sidelines.' He shrugged his grey, shirt-clad shoulders. 'But I suppose we made a bit of a hash of it the other night.' Tom's eyes grew eager. 'Anyway, to get down to business.' He produced a brown envelope from his back pocket, extracting a sheaf of photos. 'I staked out the Beachcomber in a borrowed van a couple of nights ago, and used a long-distance lens. I managed to get some shots of Lambert arriving at the pub at about seven-thirty. Some of the pictures are a bit blurry, but one or two aren't bad.'

'Yes,' Lily agreed, sifting through the photographs. 'You can clearly see Lambert's face in that one, and I recognise a couple of those other blokes, too. Lambert's heavies.' She paused, feeling slightly offended. 'I just wish you'd asked me along, Tom.'

'Too risky. I don't want to put you in any more danger than is absolutely necessary.'

'Oh.' Lily felt gratified at his concern, as Tom put the photographs back in his pocket. 'I can look after myself, though.'

'I'm sure you can. Well, maybe you can come along with me next time. I've been doing

31

a bit of homework on our mate, Gerry, as well,' Tom went on.

'That's funny, because I have, too. Come on then, Mr Hotshot Reporter, let's compare notes. You go first.' She leaned closer across the small pub table and, inadvertently, her knee brushed against Tom's.

'Well, our man is known as Gerry "The Coat" Lambert,' Tom explained, seeming not to notice the warmth stealing up Lily's cheeks. Tom lowered his voice as he continued, 'Apparently, our Mr Lambert is part of a major Brighton criminal gang . . .'

'Yes, so I'd gathered.' Lily was unable to keep quiet any longer. 'I went to the library last night, and looked through some old newspapers. Lambert's been up in court several times over the years, but they've never quite managed to nail him. The charges have included receiving stolen property, grievous bodily harm, and extortion.'

'Nice,' Tom commented ironically, toying with a beer mat. 'From what I hear, he's also involved in some not-quite-legit business, too. According to my contacts, he runs a nifty little sideline as a loan shark, as well as being a property landlord. Dabbles in the motor trade, too. Nasty bit of work, by all accounts. So,' he asked, changing the subject, 'what did you think of my mate, Jamie?'

For the second time in half an hour, Lily found herself flushing. She bowed her head over her drink, letting her hair fall forward.

'Well, he seemed nice enough, I suppose.'

Tom raised one eyebrow at her.

'I see.'

For a moment, in the crowded, noisy pub, it was as if a shadow seemed to pass across her face.

To make conversation, Lily said, 'How do you know him?'

After a fraction of a second, Tom's face relaxed into its usual, easygoing expression.

'Oh, the two of us go back a long, long way. We were at school together. Jamie's a few months younger than me. He's a bit like the younger brother I never had, being an only child.'

The pub doors banged open. Lily saw Jamie come in. After a couple of moments, he spotted them and came over. A wide grin split his face. Lily found her heart beating faster.

'Hello, mate.' Tom's expression mirrored his friend's delight. 'Success, I take it?'

Jamie nodded as he looked from Tom to Lily. He grabbed a stool with one hand, dragging it towards him.

'I'll tell you both all about it. First of all I thought I'd get into character, blend in with the scenery, you know. So I went into the pub and had a drink. Then, as luck would have it, the landlord, Mr Lambert, as I correctly suspected, was having a bit of bother with a rowdy drunk, so I went over and helped him

33

escort the drunk from the pub . . .'

'Clever,' Lily said admiringly, her eyes drifted towards Jamie's impressive biceps. She snatched her gaze back towards his face. 'So, without really trying, you managed to gain Lambert's confidence.'

'Yeah,' Jamie replied modestly, 'well, it was more luck than judgement.'

'So, then,' Jamie continued, playing to an enthralled audience, 'I got chatting to Lambert, told him I'd just moved to the area. Then I said, "I've got some booze in the car. I'll go and get it, shall I?"'

'What did Lambert say?' Tom queried.

'He asked me how much I had. Seemed to think I was on the level, didn't seem at all suspicious or anything. I told him my name was Jimmy Donovan, but he didn't ask who I was. Then, when Lambert found out it was vodka, he was even more pleased. He said he could dilute it, make even more money out of the punters.'

Lily and Tom exchanged glances.

'So,' Lily pressed, 'did he pay you with dodgy bank notes?'

Jamie nodded, and said, 'He'd taken me through to this back roam by then. He told me he would buy my dodgy booze if I would take some of his fake notes.'

'So did you manage to find anything else out?' Tom's own expression was stonily unamused.

34

'Well,' Jamie replied, 'I probed carefully, if you know what I mean. Gerry Lambert and his cronies were telling me that the notes came from a printer, this old bloke at some secret address, somewhere in the East Sussex area. Apparently, it involves a big machine and computer software. It's quite a tricky business these days, producing a credible fake note, so they said.'

'Yes, it must be hard conning innocent people like my father,' Lily said.

'The thing is, they have to tackle a holographic foil,' Jamie continued, unperturbed, 'and colours designed to combat scanning.'

'Yes,' Lily admitted. 'I had a look on the Internet the other night, and found out something similar.'

With a brief nod of acknowledgment, Jamie went on, 'Then there's a silver thread, and the watermark, to reproduce. Anyway,' he concluded, shrugging, 'I thanked the blokes, took the money, and told them I might be seeing them again in the not-too-distant future. Here, look.'

Beneath the table, Jamie fanned out an impressive array of twenty-pound notes, fake twenty-pound notes.

'That's more than we got the other day, isn't it, Tom? They look good, don't they? You can hardly tell they're not real,' Lily said.

Tom clapped his friend on the back and

said, 'Yes, well done, mate. You've given us something to get our teeth into there. Now, if you don't mind . . .' He took the notes deftly from Jamie, who exclaimed indignantly.

'Sorry, mate, those aren't for spending.' Tom pocketed the notes. 'I'll need to hang on to them, for evidence.' He rubbed his long-fingered hands together in anticipation, and a journalist's enthusiasm lit his eyes. 'I can see this has got the making of a great little exposé, maybe even a whole series of articles.'

'Hang on a minute, aren't you forgetting something?' Lily interrupted. 'More important than your prized article, we might actually get close to nailing Gerry Lambert and his slimy cronies, and stop them cheating innocent people out of a living!'

'Of course,' Tom replied coolly, eyeing her. 'We'll hand the notes, and all the other evidence, into the police when we've got enough dirt on Lambert. I hadn't forgotten the other purpose of our investigation, Lily.'

Lily murmured, 'Could have fooled me.' A spark of friction shot between her and Tom as she wondered if they had different personal agendas. Lily paused, 'By the way, I think you've done brilliantly, Jamie.'

'Hey, steady on,' Tom interrupted drily. 'You'll make the man big-headed. I've never heard you speak so warmly of anyone before, Lily.' He turned to Jamie. 'Congratulations, James, you seen to have thawed our resident ice maiden.'

Lily flinched, aware that there was a grain of truth in what Tom said.

'What's the matter?' she asked him, across the pub table. 'Are you jealous because Jamie's done so well tonight, whereas, when you tried to get in with Lambert's gang, you made a mess of things?'

'I shouldn't flatter yourself, Lily,' Tom retorted, his tone harder than usual. 'It doesn't really bother me whether I have your good opinion or not.'

'I never said it did.' Lily's cheeks glowed shamefully.

'Hey, you two,' Jamie broke in, like a parent breaking up a fight between two five-year-olds. 'That's enough!'

'Anyway, like I was saying, I'm undeterred by your criticisms, Ms Mason,' Tom went on, sounding more like his normal self once again. 'Because as a matter of fact I've got something else up my sleeve.'

'Ooh, very mysterious.' Lily tucked back a lock of blonde hair.

But Tom remained stubbornly silent, simply tapping the chiselled line of his nose in an infuriating gesture. That nose looked as if it had once been broken, Lily noticed. Somehow, that slight crookedness added to the attraction of Tom's face.

'All in good time, you'll find out all in good time,' he said, annoyingly.

37

'As long as this plan continues to require my services, Tommy, mate, I don't really mind what it entails,' Jamie said.

Lily shook her head disbelievingly.

'You honestly don't mind putting yourself in danger?'

Jamie shook his head. 'Adds to the spice of life. Anyway, to tell you both the truth,' he confided, leaning closer, resting his biceps on the table's surface, 'I'm a bit strapped for cash at the moment. I went for an audition last week, got down to the last two, but in the end it went to the other chap.'

'Don't worry, Jamie,' Tom assured his friend. 'You'll get your money. And, going on the performance you put in tonight, I'm sure you'll star in a big Hollywood movie opposite Julia Roberts one of these days.'

'I wish! Anyway,' Jamie said, scraping back his stool, 'the night is young, so, another drink, anyone?'

'Not for me thanks, Jamie,' Lily said. She glanced at her watch. 'It's getting late and I've got to be up at half past four for the newspaper delivery tomorrow.'

'I'm fine, too, thanks,' Tom said. 'I know I'm driving home, but don't overdo it, mate,' he warned, as Jamie disappeared to the bar.

Lily wondered why Tom chose to watch over Jamie like this, but the thought disappeared as quickly as Tom's friend.

When Jamie had gone, Tom turned to Lily.

38

'Uh, Lily?' For the first time since she had known him, there was a slight awkwardness in his expression.

'Yes?'

'About the other night . . .'

Lily felt the ever-present flush colour of her cheeks. Unable to meet Tom's eyes, she glanced down at the grain of the table.

'Well, I didn't exactly plan for the two of us to kiss, and I don't want you to think I was taking advantage of you.'

'No, of course I don't think that,' Lily replied quickly. 'I'm sure Lambert would have rumbled us if you hadn't kissed me at that moment.'

'That's not to say it was unpleasant,' Tom went on, as Lily raised her eyes to his.

'No.' The word of agreement had passed Lily's lips, before she knew it.

'No?' Tom seemed surprised and gratified at her agreement. 'Well,' he went on, 'I was wondering if maybe one night you would like to come . . .'

The moment was broken, as Jamie returned to the table.

'It's not as if I'm driving, Dad,' he joked. 'A couple more won't hurt.'

Exasperated at being interrupted, Tom sent Jamie a look of thunder.

'Hey, what've I done?' Jamie asked, his pale blue eyes innocent beneath the striking black brows.

'Nothing, Jamie, nothing,' Tom said resignedly, with one more look at Lily. 'As for the drinking, I'm sure you know your own limits.'

'I do. So, anyway, Lily,' Jamie went on 'how about if you and I hook up one evening? Brighton's nightlife has a lot to offer, as I'm sure you know.'

'Well, thanks for the offer, but I don't know . . .' Jamie was gazing at her so expectantly and appealingly, that Lily was tempted to accept. She couldn't help wondering, though, what Tom had been about to say to her when Jamie had interrupted.

'Go on, Lily,' Jamie prompted. 'We'll have a good time, don't you worry about that.'

Well, Lily supposed she did get on better with Jamie than with Tom.

'OK, then,' she replied. 'That would be nice.' Jamie smiled at her, she smiled back, and her heart leaped. Then, strangely, Lily felt a sudden, inexplicable flash of foreboding, which she quickly banished.

Tom looked distracted and moody. He said, drily, 'I'll be in touch with you two lovebirds about the arrangements for what we do next.'

'Hey, not so much of the lovebirds, Tom. Jamie and I are just friends,' Lily said indignantly. She glanced at Jamie. 'I don't want anything to complicate this investigation.'

'Whatever,' Tom said.

CHAPTER FOUR

Colin Bruce, the editor of the Brighton Clarion, was a plumpish man in his mid-forties, with dark-brown hair streaked with grey. He faced Tom across his cluttered desk and said, 'I called you in here, Tom, to ask how the investigation's going. You know, the fake notes, and all that.'

'The investigation's going fine, thanks, Colin,' Tom replied briefly, lounging back in his chair.

'Fine?' Colin's eager grey eyes looked like they were about to pop out of his head. 'Fine? Is that all you've got to say? Surely you've got more to report than that.'

Tom glanced through the room's glass walls, at the bustling newspaper office outside, from which they were sealed off into tranquillity.

'I told you, I've got my actor mate involved, and that seems to be going well. I've got something in mind, Col,' Tom replied slowly, 'but you know me, I like to play my cards close to my chest. Suffice it to say that I'll be requiring the loan of your Range Rover again.' He straightened in his seat. 'You'll find out why, soon enough.'

Colin sighed and said, 'Just don't go getting yourself into any trouble will you. I know what you're like. And that Lambert's a nasty bit of work.' He smoothed a hand across his sweaty brow. 'This story is potentially a big 'un, and I don't want you to blow it. Like I said before, this is one we could sell to the tabloids.'

Tom left the office, emerging into the hustle and bustle of the open-plan area. As he sat down at his computer, he tried to think about Gerry Lambert, but instead found himself thinking, again, about Lily. He hadn't seen her for several days, just spoke to her on the phone, keeping her up to speed with developments, telling her how Jamie had twice been back to the Beachcomber, with more boxes of dodgy vodka. Meanwhile, Tom and Lily had plotted what their next move would be.

She was certainly attractive, Lily, he couldn't deny that. But, after he'd split up with his wife, Tom had always vowed that it would have to be someone pretty special for him to get that involved, ever again. She was a bit too cool, as well, for his tastes, too similar to himself, some might say, although that coolness did make him want to see what lay beneath her composure . . .

'So, where are we going tonight?' Lily asked Jamie, as they sped along in a taxi the following Saturday evening. Butterflies were dancing the quickstep in her stomach, and she wondered at this strange, alien circle of acquaintances she had been drawn into. She still didn't know much about Jamie, or Tom, for that matter.

'Oh, just a little place I know,' Jamie replied, a grin lighting up his roguish face. To Lily's surprise, he got the taxi-driver to drop them at the end of Prince Regent Street, which they then walked along until they were nearly at the Beachcomber pub.

Lily turned to him, blue eyes wide.

'Please tell me we're not going to the Beachcomber.'

Jamie shook his head, laughing. 'No, don't worry. It's my night off tonight. I thought I'd bring you here.' They stopped at the building next door to the Beachcomber, the garishly-lit Atlantis Casino.

'Oh,' Lily murmured. 'Tom and I noticed this place the other night.'

'Yeah,' Jamie replied, 'I noticed it one night on my way out of the Beachcomber, too. I went along to the pub the Friday before last, you know, for a drink, and to try and familiarise myself with the locals, then.' He grinned appealingly. 'I got tempted in by the casino on my way home.'

'Oh, I see. Funny,' Lily added, looking across at sporty, designer-clad Jamie. 'I wouldn't have guessed you were a gambling man.' A blue neon dolphin flashed above their heads and Lily felt a shiver of foreboding.

'Well,' Jamie replied, 'like I said the other night, I'm a bit strapped for cash, and, you know, any chance to make a quick buck . . .'

'Make money? At a casino?' They paused at the doors, near the bouncers in their dark suits. 'You'll be lucky, Jamie!'

The corners of Jamie's mouth curled as he said, 'Don't worry,' putting a quick arm around her shoulders. 'I'll look after you.'

'You sound like Tom,' Lily commented. She wondered what Tom was doing right now, at this time on a Saturday night . . .

Jamie's eyes seemed to darken.

'Let's not talk about Tom, eh, shall we? Just for tonight?'

'That suits me just fine,' Lily replied.

One of the bouncers greeted Jamie, and they went in. The ambiently-lit interior with mirrored walls wasn't as glamorous or as intimidating as Lily had feared.

Jamie ordered a whisky from a waitress. Politely, Lily declined a drink.

'Go on, live dangerously,' Jamie coaxed Lily, as he handed the croupier some notes. 'Have a little flutter.' The female croupier took Jamie's notes, pushing them down a slot, so that they disappeared before Lily could blink. The woman in a green waistcoat handed Jamie his chips, and he passed some on to Lily.

'If you insist,' Lily murmured, with a half-smile. Ever-cautious, she decided to hedge her bets by covering four different numbers and, to her surprise, as the wheel spun and the ball clattered into a hole, one of them came up.

'Yes! I've won fifty pounds! Beginner's luck,' Lily added, collecting her chips from the croupier. 'Anyway,' she muttered to Jamie, 'I know it's a fluke. I think I'll quit while I'm ahead.'

Jamie frowned. He hunched over the gambling table. From her seat beside him, Lily gazed at the back of his head. The close-cropped, crew-cut black hair looked almost like velvet, and she felt a sudden, irrational urge to touch it.

'Oh, no!' Jamie exclaimed, as he made another loss. He took a distracted swig of his whisky.

Lily couldn't help murmuring anxiously, 'I tried to tell you gambling doesn't pay, Jamie.'

'It's OK,' Jamie replied. He slid a casual arm around her waist, speaking close into her ear. Lily shivered with traitorous pleasure. 'They know me here, Lily. They'll give me credit.'

'They know you?' Lily asked, pulling slightly back, but still within the circle of Jamie's embrace. She frowned. 'How do they know you?'

'Well,' Jamie admitted sheepishly, drawing her close again, 'firstly because I've taken to coming in here most nights over the past week or so. And secondly, because they recognise me from the pub.'

Lily gazed at him in shock. 'From the

45

Beachcomber?' she hissed.

'Yeah, that's right. I reckon the same blokes must run this place, too.'

'Well,' Lily whispered, suddenly frightened, 'you might have told me that before I agreed to come in here, Jamie!'

'Don't worry,' Jamie murmured in her ear. 'They won't recognise you.' Jamie released her from his embrace. He stroked her arm. She had the feeling that she was being watched.

No sooner had Jamie asked for more chips on credit, than one of the suit-clad bouncers materialised at his elbow. Jamie glanced up.

'Would you mind following me a moment, sir?'

Wariness flared in Jamie's eyes. He got to his feet.

'OK . . .' Lily moved to follow him, but Jamie laid a hand on her arm. 'It's all right, Lil. I won't be a minute. You wait here.'

Lily watched anxiously as Jamie followed the bouncer off to a discreet doorway near the rear of the casino. The door closed behind both men. Where was Jamie being taken?

*   *   *

Gerry Lambert sat at a desk in the back-room, a couple of sidekicks beside him, whom Jamie thought he recognised. To one side of the room was a bank of TV screens, on which was

46

playing live footage of scenes around the casino, from the CCTV cameras. Jamie caught sight of Lily on one of the cameras, and his stomach shifted uneasily.

Gerry Lambert used Jamie's false name.

'Now, Jimmy, my son, I'm a reasonable man, as my two friends here will tell you.' The two sidekicks grunted their concurrence. 'I instructed my staff to give you credit because you and I have done business together at the Beachcomber next door.' Lambert leaned forward on the desk. 'But it has come to my attention, Jimmy, that you've been taking advantage of my good nature, running up a sizeable account here at the Atlantis.'

Jamie swallowed uncomfortably. He drew himself up to his full six feet, flexing his muscles.

'Have I, Gerry, Mr Lambert? That is regrettable. I can assure you that I'll settle my account, as soon as I get on a winning streak. I've just had a run of bad luck lately, that's all.'

Lambert raised an eyebrow.

'Bad luck? That doesn't extend to the ladies though, does it Jimmy?' He glanced towards a CCTV screen. 'I see you're with a very pretty girl tonight. Can't help thinking I recognise her, though.'

Quickly, Jamie changed the subject.

'You'll get your money, don't worry, Mr Lambert.' He moved to leave. 'And now, if you don't mind, I must be . . .'

Instantly, one of his sidekicks had materialised at Jamie's side, blocking his way.

'Not so fast, Jimmy, my son,' Lambert said, his tone hardening. He leaned closer, over the desk. 'Who do you work for, Jimmy?' he leered, menacingly. 'Who supplies you with the vodka?'

'What do you mean?' Jamie asked, trying to sound nonchalant.

Lambert laughed while saying, 'Come on. You're clearly the brawn of the operation, not the brains.' Inwardly, Jamie bristled, but he said nothing. 'You're just the middleman,' Lambert went on. 'And we want to cut you out.' The last three words had such a sinister edge that Jamie started to feel sick. 'Let's see how tough you really are, shall we?'

The other sidekick, a burly, shaven-headed man, produced a large tool-box from underneath the desk. He got out a bolt-cutter, flexing it recklessly.

The shaven-headed man laughed and replaced the bolt-cutter in the box. He lifted out a disc-cutter and started it up, the blade whizzing round.

Jamie shrank away. This was turning into a bad dream.

'Hey, mate,' he said quickly, 'I'm sure we can sort this all out.'

From behind the desk, Lambert spoke.

'I'll ask you again, Jimmy, who do you work for?'

'OK, OK, I'll tell you,' Jamie blurted, guiltily aware of his disloyalty. 'But this isn't what it seems.' The disc-cutter abruptly subsided into silence, and Jamie's fear ebbed slightly. 'I'm working for a mate, Tom McCleod. He's a reporter with the Brighton Clarion, and he's doing an investigative piece on counterfeit notes in the area.' Jamie hesitated, glancing toward the TV screen again. 'The girl who's with me tonight is Lily Mason. She's in on it, too. She's got a personal axe to grind because her father's business has suffered because of all the counterfeit notes going around.'

*   *   *

'Jamie!' Lily exclaimed, leaping up out of her chair as she saw him striding across the casino towards her. Impulsively she hugged his broad, muscular form. 'Thank goodness you're back,' she murmured. Noticing Jamie's pale face, she went on, 'Are you OK?'

Jamie managed a smile, his arm still around her from the hug.

'I'm fine, Lily,' he muttered into her hair. 'But let's go now, shall we?'

'Yes, let's,' Lily agreed, eager to be out of that place. 'Oh, I almost forgot,' she added on the way out. 'I'd better collect my winnings.'

They left the casino together, Lily clutching her winnings, two £20 notes and a £10 note.

Gazing across at Jamie's shaken expression, she felt that most of the pleasure had gone out of the win now. Still, she was relieved to be out of that place.

'What did they want with you?' Lily asked Jamie, as they walked off down the busy street.

'Oh, nothing much,' Jamie replied airily. 'They just wanted to, um, discuss my credit situation.'

'I see.' His tone sounded convincing, but Lily reminded herself that he was an actor by profession.

'Congratulations on your win, by the way,' Jamie added, grinning suddenly.

Lily glanced down at the notes in her hand, fanning them out.

'Hey,' she exclaimed, peering closer. 'One of those twenties looks a bit dodgy to me.'

She handed Jamie the note for his opinion, and he stroked its surface thoughtfully and said, 'You could be right.'

Lily's eyes darkened beneath her fringe.

'Maybe the Atlantis helps launder the dodgy notes,' she mused. 'By slipping fakes into the payouts?'

'Maybe.' Jamie didn't look as excited as she was by her discovery. Instead, he looked distracted.

'Jamie?' she prompted gently.

Suddenly, he stopped walking and encircled Lily in his muscular arms. He leaned forward

50

and kissed her firmly but tenderly on the lips.

Lily felt a tingle of pleasure. Strangely, though, she found herself thinking of Tom, and pulled away before the kiss could deepen.

'Let's take things slowly shall we, Jamie?' she asked quietly, gazing up into his eyes. Traffic surged by on the road beside them as she voiced her innermost thoughts. 'I've only just come out of a long-term relationship and I'm scared of rushing into something.'

Jamie's face showed a flicker of disappointment, but he nodded understandingly.

CHAPTER FIVE

The following day, Sunday, Lily was helping her father in the shop when her mobile phone rang in the back room. Her father's long-term assistant, Paul, was there, too, stacking shelves.

To Lily's surprise, it was Tom.

'Hello, stranger,' she greeted his voice on the other end.

Tom chuckled drily down the phone.

'I'm glad to hear that Jamie got you back in one piece.'

Lily thought back to the previous night's eventful date with Jamie, and said feelingly, 'Yes, just about. He took me to the Atlantis Casino, you know, the one next to the Beachcomber?'

'The Atlantis?' Tom echoed, sounding cross. 'So Jamie's back on the gambling, is he?'

'Yes, well, he certainly seemed to be a regular there. And did you know the Atlantis was connected to the Beachcomber?'

'No,' Tom said sharply. 'I think we should meet up, Lily. We need to talk properly. That's what I was ringing you about, actually.'

'This is nice,' Lily said, as they strolled along the seafront that evening, the warm breeze gently blowing their hair. The sun was a huge gold disc in the sky, hanging above the green promenade railings.

'You're easily pleased, Lily,' Tom quipped.

Lily smiled. She had been surprised at how pleased she was to see Tom again, after nearly two weeks.

'I've been in so many pubs lately,' she replied, 'I was starting to get a bit sick of them.'

They came to Brookfields Pleasure Park. Lily glanced at the sign.

'Is this place still open?'

Tom glanced at his watch.

'It's only ten-past seven. I think it's supposed to stay open till nine, as it's summer.'

They strolled in through the gates.

'How's your dad?' Tom asked suddenly, to her surprise.

Lily's eyes lit up eagerly and she said, 'He's doing really well, thanks, Tom, except when we get a dodgy note in at the shop. Then you can actually see his blood pressure shoot up. Dad's due to go and stay with my brother, Sean, and his family up in Yorkshire next week, and I think that'll be just what he needs. He's been working in the shop most days, with me and Paul keeping a firm eye on him of course, and it seems to have given him a bit of his old zest for life back.'

Her ponytail blowing in the breeze, Lily went on, 'Because the shop closed early today

53

he thought he might venture down to his local for a swift half. I told him that was OK, as long as it really was just a half.' Her mouth twisted with worry. 'After that he's strictly on the fruit juice, doctor's orders.'

'Never mind the doctor. I should think Eddie's terrified of disobeying you!' Tom said with a grin. His floppy brown hair glinted gold where it caught the sun. 'You sound like a pretty hard taskmaster to me.'

He leaned closer to her as he teased, and Lily was reminded of the crackle of attraction between them. She looked away, as they followed the winding Tarmac path through the park's landscaped hills, crossing the miniature railway track and making for the ornamental lake.

'So,' Tom asked, seeming to grow more distant again, 'how did the date with Jamie go last night?'

'It wasn't a date,' Lily replied, starting to feel defensive. Lately, she seemed to be constantly defending herself in this way. 'And, yes, to answer your question, it went fine, thank you, Tom.' Despite everything, she had enjoyed herself, and wondered if Jamie would remain true to his promise to ask her out again. 'Anyway, that reminds me,' she went on, her voice growing in eagerness. 'Jamie didn't seem to be doing too well on the gambling, but lady luck was smiling on me, and I had a modest win, fifty pounds!'

'Good for you.' Tom raised an eyebrow, as a family of swans sailed past them. 'But why are you telling me, Lily? Planning to take me out to dinner on the proceeds?'

Lily flicked him gently on the arm.

'No, I'm afraid not. I think my dad deserves a treat more than you. I'm telling you, Tom . . .' Her eyes lit up. '. . . and this is the exciting part, because one of the twenty-pound notes in my winnings was a fake!'

She scrabbled in her shoulder bag, getting the fake note out of her purse. She passed it to Tom for his inspection.

'Definitely a fake,' Tom agreed avidly, handing the note back to her.

Lily went on, 'Now, like I said on the phone, I found out from Jamie that Lambert owns the casino as well as the Beachcomber.'

Thoughtfully, Tom finished the sentence for her. 'So they use the Atlantis to launder the fake notes.'

'My thoughts exactly!' Lily exclaimed, and their eyes locked. 'Funny,' she went on, chewing her lip, 'when I told Jamie of my theory, he didn't seem quite so excited.'

'Well, Jamie's a laid-back kind of guy, I suppose.' Glancing at her, Tom went on, 'Didn't you feel at all concerned about going into the Atlantis, Lily? Weren't you worried that Lambert might recognise you?'

Lily said, 'I was a little bit concerned. The management called Jamie in to have a word about his credit situation, but apart from that nothing untoward happened and the evening passed without incident.'

'Well, that's fortunate.' Tom's eyes darkened. 'Jamie's a good mate but he's an idiot sometimes. He should know better than to succumb to that nasty little habit of his again.'

They had come full circle round the lake and all the fresh air was starting to make Lily sleepy.

'I must say,' Tom drawled, 'I've never made a woman yawn before.'

Lily laughed and said, 'It's not you, Tom. You're not that boring, honestly.' Tom light-heartedly grabbed her wrists, pulling her towards him. Still laughing, Lily tugged herself free. 'No, seriously, it's all the early mornings, working in the shop.'

'Come on, Lily,' Tom said firmly, slipping an arm through hers, 'I'll take you home. You look like you need an early night.' They left the park and headed back down the promenade. 'And in the car on the way back, we can discuss where we're heading next with this investigation, now that you've stumbled on this interesting new lead.'

Ten minutes later, Tom pulled up in the street outside Mason's corner shop. Lily was saying, 'We still need more proof that the casino is laundering the dodgy money. Maybe Jamie and I should go back to the Atlantis and have a sniff around.' She shivered slightly at the prospect.

'If you feel safe doing that, Lily,' Tom said, turning off the ignition. He frowned. 'Are you sure no-one recognised you?'

'Sure.' A stickler for precision, she amended, 'Well, pretty sure.'

'And as long as Jamie can keep his gambling habit under control,' Tom continued. 'I don't know if it's foolhardy, encouraging him to set foot inside a casino. Although hopefully you'd be a good influence on him.'

'Hmm. Maybe.' Lily glanced up at the flat. 'Oh. There's no lights on upstairs. Dad must still be down the road at the Rose and Crown.'

'I hope he hasn't disobeyed you and had a pint instead of a half,' Tom said wryly. 'Or there'll be hell to pay.'

Lily tried to glare at Tom, but instead she found herself sharing his smile. Then, suddenly, Tom was kissing her, and she was kissing him back. It was, Lily found, very pleasant.

They pulled apart.

'Sorry,' Tom said, looking at her. 'Am I treading on Jamie's toes? I wouldn't want to do the dirty on a mate.'

'No!' Lily replied exasperatedly. 'I keep telling you, Tom. Nothing happened between the two of us yesterday evening.' She remembered the brief kiss and thought confusedly, well, more or less nothing.

57

Compelled to honesty, she said, 'Well, he did kiss me, but it was just a quick peck on the lips. I told him I wasn't ready for anything more.'

'You're not telling me that Jamie and you are just good friends?' Tom asked sceptically.

'Yes, sort of,' Lily replied uneasily. 'Like you and me are, too.'

'I don't think friends kiss like we just kissed.'

'Yes, well, maybe that was a mistake,' Lily said hesitantly. 'I don't want to lead either you or Jamie on. That's why I'd prefer it if we were friends. Anyway, thanks for this evening, Tom.' She smiled. 'I enjoyed it.'

'Me, too,' Tom said. 'I'll be in touch.'

Lily waved as Tom drove off with a wave and a roar of the engine.

She unlocked her front door and trudged upstairs to the flat, her legs suddenly leaden with tiredness. Yes, all seemed quiet, she could hear no hum of the television, so her dad must still be at the pub. As Lily walked into the kitchen she stopped dead.

'Oh, no,' she murmured. 'We've been burgled.'

The place was in disarray. Drawers were pulled out from the units, cupboards were hanging open with their contents spilling out and the kitchen chairs lay overturned on the floor. Beside the fridge-freezer was a spreading pool of water. The switch had been clicked to the OFF position.

'Dad?' she called out, hesitantly, but, as she had expected, there was no reply.

She went into the sitting-room, where a similar scene met her eyes. Toothpaste had been squirted liberally into the aperture of the video recorder, a particularly vindictive touch. Strangely, though, nothing appeared to be missing.

Lily's bedroom, too, had been ransacked. Her computer was switched on, and it looked as if someone had had a quick search through her files. Why, Lily wondered. They wouldn't find anything of interest there.

The last room she checked was the bathroom. It was filled with clouds of steam. Lily turned off the taps at the basin and bath, which had been left running. Next to her dad's shaving things, her lipstick rolled, discarded and crushed, on the tiled windowsill. Glancing up at the mirror, she saw, written in red, the words BE CAREFUL.

Suddenly, a whisper of suspicion echoed in Lily's brain.

She rushed back to the kitchen, and went to the phone. With clammy fingers, Lily dialled Tom's mobile number. Her hands shook as she waited for him to answer. The phone rang and rang, but he did not pick up. Of course, he must still be driving home, and have his phone switched off.

Ten minutes later, her father had still not

returned home. Lily tried Tom's mobile again.

'Lily.' The tone of his voice told her what he was going to say before he said it. 'I was just going to ring you. My flat's been trashed.' Tom went on, 'I think Lambert's on to us.'

'Our flat, too,' Lily heard herself saying shakily.

Tom sounded shocked and said, 'Oh, goodness, Lily. Are you OK?'

'I think so.' She half-choked on a sob. 'No. Not really. My dad's not home yet. I don't know what he's going to do when he finds out.'

'Lily,' Tom said suddenly, abruptly. 'Hang on. I'm coming round there. I'll be two ticks.' And, without further preamble, he hung up.

Lily stood, dazed, gazing at the humming receiver. It was very kind of Tom to offer to come. She felt relieved and comforted at the thought that he was on his way.

His mobile phone still in his hand, Tom McCleod stood in his bathroom and stared at his reflection in the broken mirror. He felt furious that those thugs had involved Lily in this, and furious with himself, too, because it was partly his fault that she was involved.

Ten minutes later, he arrived at the small flat above the corner shop.

'Oh, Tom,' Lily murmured in the hallway, inexpressibly glad to see his face. 'It's kind of you to come.' He hugged her, firmly and amiably. Lily squeezed him tightly back, which sent her heart thumping in her chest.

'They broke a small window in the back room to get in,' Lily said breathily, as they entered the flat. 'There's a warning written in lipstick on the bathroom mirror,' she added. 'It says, **Be Careful**.'

Tom made a short, mirthless sound.

'Ditto. Except that my mirror's been smashed and they've written across it in marker pen.'

'What have they written?'

'**Mind Your Own Business**.'

'Look in here.' Lily showed Tom the scene in the bathroom. Wordlessly, he took it in.

'They don't appear to have taken anything,' Lily said. 'What about you?'

'They've emptied the box file where I was keeping the typed notes for my articles and some of the photographs. They've taken some of the counterfeit notes, too, but luckily I've got more in my wallet for safe-keeping.'

Lily gasped. 'So all the work you've done on your article so far has been destroyed?'

'If the worst came to the worst, most of it's still in my head,' Tom said. 'I haven't lost too much of the hard evidence, there wasn't actually that much hard evidence, yet. And my notes are stored in a file on my computer at work, and saved on a disc there, too.'

As they wandered back to the chaotic sitting-room, Lily said hesitantly, 'You don't suppose they've found out where you work, too?'

Tom's cheek muscles clenched as he said, 'We'll have to report these break-ins to the police, for insurance purposes at least. We'll both need a crime number to give to our insurance companies.'

'I wonder what the police will say,' Lily asked, 'when we tell them that some gangsters trashed our homes? They might be a bit sceptical about that, especially seeing as there's no proof of who did it.'

'No, we'll just have to report this as a straightforward break-in,' Tom told her.

Lily looked up, her brow creased.

'Can't we just come clean with the police, Tom? Tell them everything?'

Tom glanced over at her.

'What, and give up the investigation before we've got enough on Lambert to nail him?' He shook his head, his face alight with what Lily now recognised as journalistic enthusiasm. 'That would be letting the crooks win.'

Lily felt uneasy and said, 'But, Tom, won't the police think it strange that the burglars didn't take anything?'

Tom replied casually, 'The fact that the supposed burglars didn't appear to take anything, apart from my research stuff, is immaterial. Maybe they didn't see anything they fancied.'

'Maybe. And I suppose I'll tell Dad it was a

simple break-in, too. He doesn't know that I'm involved with you and Jamie, Tom, let alone that I'm crossing paths with people like Gerry Lambert. I don't know what it would do to poor Dad's heart if he did know.' Lily stopped to glance at her watch. 'Heavens, it's nearly ten o'clock and he's still not back.' She frowned. 'Maybe he's decided to stay till last orders. I can't thank you enough for helping me like this, Tom. It's very good of you,' Lily added guiltily, 'when you've still got your own place to sort out.' She found she was shaking. 'You know,' Lily confessed, gesturing at the room, 'I still can't believe I've become involved in something like this. I was quite content with my safe, uneventful life.'

Tom came over and hugged her.

'It's all right, Lily, you're safe now. This is just a warning to back off. Lambert and the others wouldn't do anything to hurt you.'

Again Lily was surprised by Tom's solicitousness. She could smell his aftershave, and something indefinable. She pulled back, looking at him.

'What about you, Tom? Aren't you at all scared?'

'No.' Tom's eyes narrowed to slits. 'I'm not going to let anyone intimidate me.' He chuckled drily. 'I am a hard-bitten newshound, after all. I've seen it all before.' He glanced down at Lily, with concern. 'Are you saying you want out of the investigation, though,

Lily? Because I'd understand perfectly if you do.'

Thinking of her father, Lily shook her head firmly.

'No, I'm with you, Tom. I'm not going to be threatened by anyone.'

Tom looked doubtful. 'Well, if you're sure, Lily.' Gently, he traced the curve of her cheek with his thumb.

'You don't get rid of me that easily, Tom McCleod,' Lily replied, with a stoutness she didn't feel. 'I wonder what Jamie will make of all this,' she added, musingly, gazing past Tom to a point beyond his shoulder.

'Yes, Jamie.' Tom glanced down at Lily's unseeing gaze and his eyes darkened like a sky before rain.

CHAPTER SIX

Two days later, on the Tuesday evening, Lily and her dad were relaxing in their sitting-room over a cup of tea.

'Well, I think you should go, Lily, love,' Edward Mason said. 'A little break would do you the world of good. You might as well relax a bit, while your boss has authorised you some more time off work.'

'Yes, but that wasn't exactly the idea, Dad. I was given the unpaid leave so that I could help keep an eye on the shop for you, and look after you while you convalesced.'

Her father was mesmerised by the burbling television.

'I'm feeling so much better now, Lil. I'm hardly convalescing any more.'

'I know, and that's great.' He'd even handled the news of the break-in better than Lily had expected. 'But there's no way I'd feel happy leaving you on your own just yet.'

His blue eyes lighting up, Eddie played his trump card.

'I phoned Sean earlier. Asked him if I could come up to them a few days early, midweek. He and Sally said that would be fine. I checked with Paul and Nathan, and they can cover for me here, and generally keep an eye on the place. So I thought, if it's OK with you,

I'd travel up to Yorkshire tomorrow.'

'Oh.' Lily cursed inwardly. So her father had brought forward his week's stay with her brother, Sean, and his family. For some reason, she had been looking for an excuse not to take up Tom's offer of what, in his mind at least, passed for a holiday.

Tom had phoned her that morning at half-six, before she opened up the shop, and it was unfortunate that her father had wandered into the shop halfway through the conversation. At least he hadn't heard the first part, though.

'Lambert's men have been to the newspaper offices as well,' Tom had greeted her, in a low, terse voice.

Lily's heart lurched unpleasantly. She glanced around her.

'Are you there now, Tom? At the office?'

'That's right. So you'll appreciate, it's quite difficult to elaborate.'

'So no-one else there knows yet, then?' Lily asked in surprise.

'No, and as far as I'm concerned, that's the way it'll stay,' Tom replied. 'I know how these people operate,' he muttered. 'It was an expert break-in. They don't want to draw attention to this sort of place, or the police will be on to them.'

Lily glanced anxiously through to the busy shop, aware that her services were required, and soon she would have to go and turn the shop's sign to OPEN.

'I've been worrying, Tom,' Lily blurted out, suddenly feeling that she was in too deep. 'And now, after what you've just told me, I'm even more worried. Can't we just go to the police?'

'What, and give up the investigation, let them get away with it?' Tom asked indignantly. 'No, I've got a better idea. I think we should lie low for a while, get out of the area. How about you and I go down to Bournemouth for a few days, Lily? I think we could both do with a little holiday.'

'A holiday?' Lily asked bemusedly. Suddenly she was aware that her father had appeared in the back room. Eddie busied himself with the kettle. 'Thanks for the offer, but I don't think so, Tom,' Lily replied. No, there was no way she could leave Eddie on his own here, with Lambert on the prowl.

'Think about it,' Tom said quickly, forestalling her protests. 'Look, I've got to go now, Lily, and I know you're busy, too. I'll call you later.' And with that he had hung up.

It was only now, later that evening, that Lily remembered that her dad had overheard part of that morning's conversation.

'So I'll be up at Sean's and Sally's by tomorrow evening,' he said from his armchair, his blue eyes twinkling. 'So you can get away for a nice break with your new man-friend, Tom, wasn't it, with a clear conscience.'

Lily couldn't help smiling at the quaint expression.

'He's not my man friend, Dad. And besides, are you sure you're feeling up to travelling to Yorkshire? It's a long way.'

'I'll be fine on the train,' Eddie said robustly.

At that moment, on cue, the phone rang. It was Tom on the other end, asking her again to come away to Bournemouth with him.

And Jamie, despite his promises, had yet to ring her . . .

Anyway, what Tom proceeded to tell her over the phone only confirmed Lily's inclinations. He told her that, at that precise moment, from the window of his flat, he could see an unfamiliar car parked in the street outside, with two men in it, lurking in a sinister fashion.

'So you see, Lily,' his husky voice finished, 'I really think it would make sense for us to get away for a while, soon.'

'How soon do you mean exactly?'

'Tomorrow.'

Hesitantly, wondering what she was getting herself into, Lily found herself agreeing.

At ten-thirty the next morning, Tom's car was waiting but, as she approached it, Lily was stunned to see the Range Rover parked behind it, with Jamie sitting in the driving seat. Jamie waved a hand.

'What's this?' Lily asked, as Tom came to

take her rucksack from her. 'Is Jamie coming, too?'

Tom, casually dressed as ever, in jeans and a faded grey cotton shirt, looked nonplussed.

'Yes.' He frowned. 'Sorry, Lily, didn't you realise? I agree,' he went on, with a sudden grin that turned her insides to jelly, 'that it would have been more pleasant if it'd just been the two of us.' He cast such a look in the direction of the Range Rover that Lily wondered if Jamie had done something to offend Tom. 'But Jamie's in this as deep as we are, and I think it's important that he gets away, too. We're going to drive down in convoy.'

So much for that romantic break for two, Lily thought, feeling foolish as she got into Tom's car. Then they roared off, with Jamie following, leaving the likes of Gerry Lambert far behind them.

'What about those men?' Lily asked, as they headed off along the coast road. 'The ones that were hanging around outside your flat last night? The ones you thought might be Lambert's men?'

'They'd gone by this morning,' Tom said, concentrating on the road ahead. 'As far as I'm concerned, it was a further threat to leave well alone.'

Lily glanced around over her shoulder, at the Range Rover following them. Turning back to Tom she frowned.

'Did Lambert's men wreck Jamie's place, too?'

'No, apparently not.'

'Oh,' Lily replied, glancing at Tom's selection of CDs and wondering if he would let her play one. 'Well, that's something, at least. What's Jamie doing in your boss's Range Rover?' Lily asked.

Tom gripped the wheel a little tighter.

'Oh,' he said offhandedly, 'I thought he'd better look the part, just in case we stumbled across any new leads to follow up down there.'

'Any new leads?' Lily echoed indignantly. 'I thought this was supposed to be a holiday, Tom, a chance to get away from it all.'

Tom glanced briefly across at her, with a flash of a reassuring smile.

'It is, Lily. And don't worry, I'll look after you.' He shook his head as he turned back to the road. 'All right, Lily. I have been given a new lead on Lambert's gang to follow, over in Bournemouth. It could lead us to conclusive proof on our man.'

'Well, I'm not sure you really need me on this trip, anyway,' she retorted, turning to look frostily out of the window. 'I'm only the poor sop who's on some desperate, misguided mission to save her father's business.'

Suddenly, before Lily realised what was happening, Tom had pulled the car off the seafront road, into a lay-by. He turned to her, raising a finger to touch her cheek, using the

70

finger to turn her face towards him.

'I wanted you to come, Lily. And not just because I didn't think it'd be safe for you in Brighton at the moment.' He paused. 'I like you, Lily, and I enjoy your company. I wanted you to come on the trip with me.'

Lily felt herself blushing hotly.

'I expect you're used to charming women, aren't you, Tom McCleod?' she asked, to hide her discomposure. 'But the facts are still the same, by embarking on this trip, we seem to be leaping out of the frying-pan, into the fire.' Her eyes darkened to sapphire.

'I'll take you home if that's what you want, Lily. Just say the word.'

'No,' Lily muttered, some of her anger subsiding. Part of her couldn't help being excited that Tom had a new lead on Lambert's gang. 'You might as well drive on, now we've started. Besides, I don't fancy sticking around on my own to face Lambert.' She was silent for a couple of minutes as Tom revved up the car again and pulled back on to the road. Finally, curiosity compelled Lily to add, 'What is this lead, anyway?'

Four and a half hours later, they had arrived at Bournemouth. Tom pulled up outside a hotel in a hilly street parallel to the seafront.

'We've got three single rooms,' he said, unclipping his seatbelt.

'They'll think that's a rather odd set-up,'

71

Lily mused.

'Not really,' Tom replied, opening his door and getting out. He stuck his head back in. 'We could be business colleagues. I suppose we are, really.'

Having made no mention of the more personal side of their relationship, he slammed the car door behind him.

Lily watched Jamie, who had emerged from the Range Rover, jog up to approach Tom. The two men proceeded to have a brief consultation on the pavement.

Lily observed the two tall, good-looking men. In contrast to Tom's jeans and stylish faded shirt, Jamie's jeans were teamed with his customary sporty designer wear and a hooded top and a baseball cap. Then, as Tom headed towards the Hotel Sunshine, Jamie turned back and came towards the car.

'How're you doing, Lily?'

Lily smiled and said, 'Fine thanks, Jamie.' Was it her imagination, or did those pale eyes look a little uneasy?

Jamie grinned, banishing the uneasy expression.

'We had a good time, didn't we, the other night? I was, uh, going to ring you to ask you out again.'

A hint of autumnal chill blew in through the window.

'It's all right, Jamie,' Lily told him. 'I haven't been sitting by the phone day and night, willing it to ring. We don't have to play games with each other, I'm sure we can discuss things like mature adults.'

Tom emerged from the hotel, bearer of the good news that there were three single rooms available. As Tom approached his car, however, what he saw made him stop dead.

There was Jamie, leaning carelessly against the side of his car, as if he, and not Tom, owned it, busy working his charm on Lily. Lily was smiling up at Jamie, and Jamie's dark head was bent solicitously towards her. A cosy little scene, Tom thought grimly. And, recalling how things had ended between him and his wife, Tom knew he had good reason to mistrust a friend.

But Tom liked Jamie, he remembered with something of a surprise, as he approached the car. He would do well to keep this in mind, and try to suppress those feelings of impatience and, dared he think it, a slight mistrust towards Jamie, which had been resurfacing more and more frequently over recent days.

Someone had spilled the beans on Lily and himself to Lambert's gang, but, no, Tom told himself, it couldn't be Jamie. It would be just too inconvenient, for starters. Tom needed Jamie. He had a vital rôle to play in this investigation.

Some time later, there was a knock on Lily's hotel room door. She, Tom and Jamie had agreed that they might as well take time to settle in today and meet up later to grab something to eat in the evening.

Now it was almost a quarter to seven, and the light was beginning to fail. Lily smoothed the creases out of her trousers and went to answer the door. Tom stood there, looking as if he, too, had refreshed himself after the long journey.

'Jamie's discovered the hotel's got a gym,' Tom announced dryly, leaning against her doorframe. 'So I expect that's the last we'll see of him for several hours.'

'Yes, well, I suppose he's got to maintain those impressive biceps somehow,' Lily murmured. Glancing at Tom's own arms, half-hidden beneath his short-sleeved shirt, she couldn't help noticing that he had pretty impressive biceps of his own. She tore her gaze away.

Tom went on, 'I told Jamie we'd meet up with him in the hotel restaurant at eight. I wondered if you fancied coming for a stroll, in the meantime.'

'I don't know,' she prevaricated. A half-teasing smile played around her lips. 'I'm still not sure if I've forgiven you for deceiving me earlier, Tom.'

'Well, I'll be straight with you this time.' Tom leaned a little closer to her in the doorway. Lily's heartbeat quickened. But Tom did not kiss her.

'My contact's given me a location to check out. I thought you and I might go and case the joint.'

Lily thought of her father's failing business. Her heart beat fast.

'I say we do it.'

The address Tom had been given seemed to be on the other side of town.

'We might as well walk,' Tom said, as they set off towards the seafront. 'It's less conspicuous and besides, it's a nice evening.'

It wasn't a bad evening, although it was September now, the kids were back at school and that autumnal chill was well and truly in the air. Tom produced a street map from his back pocket and studied it as they walked along the clifftop promenade.

The sun was melting into the sea below them, leaving a shimmering trail across the wet sand. They passed Bournemouth's pier and, in the distance, the neighbouring pier of Boscombe loomed larger.

Tom scrutinised the map.

'I think we ought to turn off here, head back into the town.'

They took a left turn, leaving the seafront behind and heading for the darkening streets inland. Recalling what Tom had told her on the journey up, Lily asked, 'So, this bloke, Lambert's brother, you say he runs a carpark?'

'Yes, that's right, Franklin Road, according to my source.'

They turned a corner and a large carpark became visible, illuminated by street lamps, flanked by grimy-looking warehouses. It was now gone seven o'clock and the carpark was deserted, its barriers closed.

'Looks like Lambert's brother doesn't take particularly good care of this place,' Lily observed, gazing at the lumpy Tarmac with the odd weed growing through, and the faded markings of the parking spaces. There was no sign of life from the dingy hut standing guard beside the barriers, a list of charges displayed on its side.

'Sidney Lambert apparently thought he'd come in on the counterfeiting scam, too,' Tom said from beside her. He walked over to the barriers and Lily followed him. 'My source tells me he moved down here a few years ago to work a different patch. Sidney's a smaller-scale villain than his big brother, but rumour has it he's not the sort of bloke you'd want to take home to meet your granny.'

Lily shivered and said, 'So does this Sidney use the carpark to launder fake money?' she whispered.

'Got it in one.' Tom scratched his chin thoughtfully. 'I'd really like to take a closer look at this place.' Suddenly he grabbed Lily's hand. 'Come on, I've got an idea.' He led her down the street, past the carpark, towards one of the dark-brick Victorian warehouses that loomed above them, its windows glinting in

76

the moonlight. A large **FOR SALE** board added to the air of dereliction. Lily followed Tom down a side alley.

'What are you doing, Tom?' she hissed anxiously.

'Just having a look round.' Tom raked a careless hand through his hair. He tried a door, and almost fell headlong into the building when it opened easily. Tom's eyes gleamed. 'Bingo!'

*   *   *

Jamie Latham's feet pounded away at the treadmill, working off some of his pent-up frustration and, yes, he had to admit, anxiety. He wished fervently now that he hadn't revealed all to Lambert about Tom and Lily, but Jamie had a vivid mental image of that thug holding the disc-cutter.

He switched off the treadmill, his steps slowing to a standstill, and went over to the bench press. This gym may be small, but at least he had it to himself.

Was he imagining it, or was there an atmosphere between him and Tom lately? Did Tom suspect? But that was why he was here. He had to keep working for Tom, not just for the much-needed money, but to repay him for the wrong he'd done, and convince him of his innocence. And he had to keep out of Gerry Lambert's way. Jamie hadn't a hope of clearing his debts, as things stood at the moment.

'Anyone at home?' Tom called, back at the warehouse, his voice echoing round the vast, bare room. Lily's heart pounded in the silence that followed. The place was in semi-darkness, due to the meagre amount of street-light coming through the grimy windows.

Tom produced a small torch from his back pocket, flicking it on. The scene was illuminated, a scattering of boxes and crates, a pile of metal pipes in the middle of the floor that had perhaps once been used to house electrical wiring.

Shivering at the eerie atmosphere, Lily said, 'Let's take a look upstairs.'

They found the first floor to be in a similar state. There were a couple of chairs, an empty cigarette packet and some old wrappers.

'Looks like we weren't the first ones here,' Lily commented.

'Shall we try the top floor?' Tom said. They climbed on up the narrow stairs to the second floor. One of the small window panes up there was broken and, as Tom flashed his torch beam around, there was a flutter of wings from the rafters. A pigeon flew towards them.

'Oh!' Lily almost jumped out of her skin.

The exclamation echoed round the empty room.

'Sorry,' she said, feeling suddenly foolish. 'I've always had a bit of a phobia about birds.'

Tom flicked off his torch, coming closer,

laying a protective arm around her shoulders. Still encircled, she turned to face him and suddenly, in the darkness, they were kissing.

As they drew apart breathlessly, Tom said huskily, 'Sorry. Couldn't resist that.' His expression was unreadable, but she could just see the glint of his eyes in the light from the moon.

The beating wings had long since stilled and Lily pulled free of the embrace, crossing the floorboards to the windows. Tom had apologised, that meant it had been a mistake. She heard Tom's footsteps behind her.

'Hey, look,' she exclaimed. 'You can see the carpark from here.'

Tom stood grimly behind her.

'Ah, yes, so you can.'

Lily turned to him, eyes wide.

'You know what I'm thinking? That this would be the ideal place . . .'

'. . . to stake out the carpark from,' Tom finished for her. 'We can take some photos from here, get a really clear picture of what Sidney Lambert's up to, plenty of evidence.'

Lily felt a tingle of fear.

'But what if Sidney discovers us up here, and informs big brother, Gerry, back in Brighton?'

'Don't worry,' Tom said, with easy assurance, 'he won't. And now,' Tom was going on, 'we'd better get back to the hotel.' He turned to her, stroking a finger down her cheek. 'And we don't want to offend Jamie just now.'

'Why?' Lily frowned, catching the finger and removing it from her cheek. 'Have you got some more work for him to do?'

Tom nodded, curling his other finger round to clasp her hand.

'Jamie's alter-ego is going to be called into action again very soon. Yes, I think it's time he introduced himself to Sidney Lambert.'

CHAPTER SEVEN

The following morning, after breakfast, Tom and Lily returned to the warehouse. No mention was made of the scene between them there the previous night, where somehow, inexplicably, Lily felt they had grown closer. Today they were armed with Tom's binoculars and state-of-the-art camera.

During the course of the morning, a handful of apparently legitimate cars arrived to park in the carpark, stopping to take a ticket from the hut first. Other cars arrived, too, their owners emerging and disappearing into the hut.

Suddenly the music to *Greensleeves* cut through the morning air.

'Good heavens!' Lily exclaimed, squinting through the binoculars. 'It's an ice-cream van!'

A stout, middle-aged man in a checked shirt got out and went into the hut. Shortly afterwards, he emerged and the van drove off.

Just after eleven o'clock, Jamie drove up in the Range Rover. Lily leaped up from her chair, the binoculars hanging around her neck.

'There he is! Bang on time.'

Lily felt a pang of fear for Jamie. They both held their breath, so close that their shoulders brushed. They watched as Jamie disappeared into the hut.

'He's been in there twenty minutes now,' Lily breathed later, starting to grow anxious. Several more long minutes passed and another man emerged from the hut, then another. Tom took more photographs. Then Jamie reappeared. He opened the boot of the Range Rover and, apparently without effort, lifted out the crate of vodka he'd bought at a supermarket that morning, disappearing back into the hut.

As Jamie lugged the crate into the dingy little hut, he had a sudden, irrational fear that word would have got out about him, from Gerry Lambert to his brother, Sidney.

The man seated behind the desk certainly seemed the suspicious type. Jamie summed him up as an ageing bruiser, with tattoos and wearing designer sportswear not unlike Jamie's own. Only the cold grey-blue eyes revealed this man to be unmistakeably a Lambert.

'There it is, then,' Jamie said, dumping the crate of vodka on the desk.

He'd certainly had to wait in line for this opportunity, following a whole string of dodgy-looking characters into the hut. This was obviously where Sidney did all his business from.

'Fell off the back of a lorry, you say?' Sidney barked, stubbing out a cigarette.

'That's right,' Jamie said casually.

The man emitted a short, dry laugh.

'Heard that one before.' A phone rang on the desk, distracting Sidney. There were two phones, Jamie noticed, as he took a seat, one black, one white. Sidney answered the black one.

'Look, mate,' he muttered into the receiver, 'can't talk now. Speak to you later.' And he hung up.

Sidney looked up again, giving Jamie that same wary, suspicious look. Finally, he glanced at the vodka, announcing in a bragging tone, 'I'll sell it all in two minutes.' Jamie heaved an inward sigh of relief, as Sidney put the crate down on the floor, then opened a desk drawer, unlocked a cash box and counted out some twenty-pound notes.

Were they fakes? Fishing for information, Jamie raised a casual black eyebrow and said, 'Those look like good quality, mate.'

Sidney grinned, revealing a gold tooth.

'They're the best, don't come cheap, mind. Eight pounds for a twenty-pound note.'

'Yeah, that does narrow the profit margin a bit.' Jamie pocketed the notes, thinking he might keep one or two back from Tom.

Now that the hut had emptied of the other various, unsavoury characters, Jamie started to relax. He leaned back in his chair.

'So do you just deal in notes, then,' Jamie asked, 'or is there a chance I can get my hands on some coins, too?'

Sidney carefully locked the cash-box.

'Funny you should mention that. I've just started my coin-making business again.' He slammed the desk-drawer closed, opened another drawer and got out a bag full of coins. 'I've got a contact, Lawrence, in Spain, for the metal mix formula.'

Jamie tried not to look too interested as Sidney spilled some coins on to the desk.

'It's a tricky business, I expect?'

'You could say that.' Sidney warmed to his subject. 'The Royal Mint use a gold-coloured security metal for pound coins, of an unknown identity. There are images in the coin, too, that only the Mint and the government know, making them particularly difficult to fake.' Sidney picked up one of the coins between his thumb and forefinger, gazing at it with pride.

'So how d'you go about it, then?' Jamie asked.

Sidney scratched his chest. 'Well,' he explained, 'you make a mould from the existing coin, then pour solder in, and coat it in gold. ' 'Course, the quality's not the same as the twenty-pound notes. 'Cos it's made from solder, the coin feels lighter than a kosher one, and if you scratch the surface . . .' He did so, with the coin he was holding, then handed it to Jamie.

'You can see grey metal underneath,' Jamie finished for him, scrutinising the coin. 'Still,' he added, 'they look convincing enough to fool most people.' Jamie broke off, suddenly distracted. 'Hang on, is that an ice-cream van I can hear?' He got up, and went over to the window. 'It's a very mild day. I wouldn't mind an ice-cream.'

Sidney laughed, a dry, mirthless cackle.

From her position at the window of the warehouse, Lily exclaimed, 'There's that ice-cream van again.' Her mouth twisted into a frown. 'There's something funny going on there.'

'Are you thinking what I'm thinking?' Tom asked.

'That Sidney Lambert is definitely using an ice-cream van to help launder his dodgy money?'

'Yes.'

'Oh, dear, Tom,' Lily said. 'Here we are, agreeing again. This is becoming a habit.'

Tom looked at her and said, 'Yes. We'll have to do something about that, won't we?' Their gazes slid back to the window.

Suddenly Lily tugged at Tom's sleeve saying, 'Now Jamie's going over to the van with another man. That must be Sidney Lambert.'

'Looks like it's ice-cream all round, then.' Tom narrowed his tawny eyes as he observed the scene. Clicking the shutter of his camera, he added, 'Hmm, I wonder just how many people are involved with this little scam.'

Ten minutes later, after witnessing more

comings and goings, they heard a door bang from somewhere below them. Lily started, her heart pounding in her chest.

'Relax,' Tom said. 'It's probably Jamie.'

Moments later there were footsteps on the stairs and Jamie's head appeared, followed by the rest of him.

'You found this place all right then,' Tom observed.

Jamie strolled over to them, with the confident swagger of someone who has completed a job successfully.

'Yeah, wasn't too much trouble.' He glanced around him. 'Mmm, nice little set-up you've got here.' His eyes came to rest on Tom and Lily, seated close together at the window, and he raised an eyebrow. 'Cosy.'

'Where did you leave the Range Rover, Jamie?' Tom asked, with a touch of sharpness, Lily noticed.

'I parked it, round the back,' Jamie added defensively.

The atmosphere between the two men seemed to be intensifying by the minute. Anxiously Lily searched for something to defuse it.

'You've got ice-cream round your mouth,' she said, as Jamie came closer.

For the first time, he almost smiled.

'Sorry I couldn't get you guys one. My new mate, Sidney Lambert, insisted on introducing me to his brother-in-law, Bert, who does a

86

nice line in ice-cream, with a side order of freshly-laundered fake coins.'

'Ah, so it's mission accomplished, is it then, Jamie?' Lily asked.

'That's right,' Jamie confirmed proudly. He pulled a sheaf of twenty-pound notes out of one pocket, and a handful of pound coins out of another. 'All fakes.'

Tom's mouth broke into a lazy smile.

'Nice work, mate,' he said, clapping Jamie on the shoulder.

'Yes, that's fantastic.' Lily gazed at the counterfeit money, then glanced up to meet those mesmerising pale blue eyes. 'I don't know what we'd do without you, Jamie.'

Was it her imagination, or did Jamie look away guiltily?

'Well, how about you meet me in the hotel bar for a drink before dinner tonight, Lily, for a chance to congratulate me properly?'

Caught off-guard, Lily blushed, and replied, 'Oh, er, OK, then.'

'Come on, Jamie,' Tom said sharply, regarding him through narrowed eyes. 'Never mind making arrangements for your social life. Aren't you going to tell us what you managed to find out?'

*　　　*　　　*

'Very nice,' Jamie said appreciatively, when Lily walked into the bar that evening. She was

87

wearing her little black dress, which she'd foolishly packed in anticipation of a mini-break for two with Tom.

'Aaah. This is nice.' Jamie set down his glass, glancing around at the ambient, subtly-lit setting, while tinkling piano music filtered softly through the sound system. He looked seriously at Lily. 'I've been meaning to do this for some time.'

'What?' Lily grinned.

Jamie leaned towards her across the table, those light blue eyes boring into her darker ones. Lily was reminded of what an attractive man he was, in that unusual, quirky way.

'Follow upon that first date we had.'

Lily was about to protest that it wasn't a date but stopped herself, not wanting to sound like a stuck record. Instead she changed the subject.

'You're right, it is a nice place here, although I can't help feeling I ought to be back in Brighton.'

'With Gerry Lambert's men lurking about?' Jamie shuddered, as if his drink tasted bad. 'You want to get that pretty head of yours testing.'

Lily pouted at Jamie.

'No, it's not that I'm desperate to get back to see Gerry. And my dad's away at the moment, staying with my brother, so I don't have to worry about that either. No,' she said thoughtfully, 'the thing is, all this is making me anxious, and I'd like to get back and hand over everything to the police.'

'The police?' Jamie echoed, looking faintly alarmed.

'Yes, but that's not all that's bothering me. I think I'm missing my job.' Her mouth twisted. 'Or rather what it represents, normal life. I've only got another week's unpaid leave after this, you see, and I'd really like to get back.'

'Yes,' Jamie agreed, pensively. 'I know what it feels like to be passionate about what you do for a living.'

Lily laughed and said, 'I can understand being passionate about something like being an actor. But I couldn't really say I was passionate about being a database administrator. I enjoy it, though.'

Suddenly Jamie had put down his drink, and his eyes had grown serious.

'I know what I am passionate about.' He leaned towards her across the glossy mahogany table as if to kiss her. Lily froze, powerless to resist.

There was a sharp cough from behind them.

'Sorry to interrupt,' Tom drawled sounding anything but.

If she'd thought Jamie scrubbed up well, Tom's appearance almost knocked the breath out of her. Like Jamie, he'd tailored his normal casual look to the demands of the occasion, and was wearing a dark, impeccably-cut linen suit, and a blue shirt.

Finally, Lily looked at his face, those long, narrow lion's eyes crinkled as if in ironic amusement. He met her gaze, and their eyes locked for a long moment.

'I hope you've got a tie for dinner, Jamie, mate,' Tom said eventually, turning to eye his friend's neck. 'Rules are rules.'

Jamie tugged the collar of his shirt. He glared resentfully at Tom.

Tom hesitated, then pulled a rolled-up dark tie from his pocket, throwing it across the table.

'Here you are.' The moment of hostility was broken.

'Oh, cheers, mate.' Jamie got to his feet. 'I think I'll go and find a mirror, put this thing on properly.'

When Jamie had gone, Tom pulled another chair up to the table. He frowned at Lily.

'What were you discussing with Jamie just then? Business?'

'Not exactly,' Lily replied. 'I was just saying how this is all very nice, but I'm feeling anxious to get back to my proper job.'

'Oh, well, hopefully it won't be long till your wish is granted.' He spoke under his breath. 'Maybe a couple more days at the warehouse and we'll have as much dirt as we need on Gerry's brother, Sidney. Then we can get back to Brighton and take the whole file to the police, and I can write my article . . .' He broke off, fiddling with a coaster. 'Anyway, like I said, I'm sorry if I interrupted anything just now.'

'Are you?' Lily challenged calmly.

Tom chewed his lip, looking uneasy.

'The thing is, Lily, I introduced you to Jamie, and I wouldn't want to be responsible for you getting involved with . . .'

'With what, Tom?' Lily demanded under her breath, suddenly anxious. 'Is there something I should know about Jamie?'

Tom looked uncomfortable and said, 'Not exactly. Nothing I can put my finger on. I've known Jamie a long time, but it's only lately that I've come to realise some things about him.'

'Like what?'

Tom sighed and went on. 'Just that he's, well, rather irresponsible, for a start. And I might be wrong, but he seems to have something on his mind at the moment. Maybe I should talk to him about it.'

Lily was about to probe Tom further, when Jamie reappeared, effectively curtailing the conversation.

*   *   *

'So Jamie's having a day in the gym today, is he?' Lily asked, as she and Tom sat in their positions in the warehouse.

'That's right,' Tom replied.

'Tom,' Lily began slowly, 'what you said yesterday, when you tried to warn me about Jamie, well, I just wanted to tell you that you needn't worry.'

Tom glanced across at her sharply, a look of surprise on his face.

'Like I told you before, I've got no intention of getting involved with your friend.'

'I know you said that before,' Tom replied tonelessly, staring out of the window. 'But, when I saw him about to kiss you, I thought things might have changed.'

'It's just so soon after I broke up with my boyfriend, Ryan. I like Jamie, and I like you. Oh, Tom,' Lily admitted, 'I'm a bit confused at the moment.'

'Do you want to talk about it?' Tom asked carelessly, from his position behind her.

'Ryan and I were together for fourteen months,' Lily heard herself saying, while she gazed down at the carpark below. 'It was fine at first. We got on really well, and planned to become engaged, but gradually he became more controlling.'

'That's outrageous,' Tom said quietly.

'So that's why I'm wary of getting involved again. And besides,' she murmured, 'Jamie's nice, but he doesn't seem right for me.'

'Lily,' Tom said seriously, 'not every man will be like Ryan. Although,' he went on, 'I can't really blame you for letting the past govern your life.' He sighed. 'I'm guilty of the same thing myself.'

Lily turned to look at him, intrigued now and said, 'Why's that?'

Tom sighed. 'Because my marriage ended when I found out my wife, Tina, was having an affair with my squash partner, David.' Tom's eyes darkened, banishing the tawny flecks.

Despite the Indian summer continuing outside, Lily felt a cold hand close around her heart. It sounded as though Tom had been deeply in love with his wife, maybe still was. Why should that bother her?

'That must have been a terrible shock,' she murmured.

Tom continued, 'I'm over it now, of course, and those two are happily settled together, running a chic Brighton wine bar, but it taught me one thing, never trust a friend.' Tom looked uncomfortable, and regretful. 'Which, I'm sorry to say, brings us back to Jamie.'

Suddenly their attention was wrenched back to the carpark below them by an ear-splitting hiss and screech of brakes.

'Oh, good heavens!' Tom exclaimed, leaping up from his chair just in time to see an articulated lorry, misjudging the corner and crashing through the barrier and into the hut, with an ominous crunch of plaster-board.

For a couple of seconds everything stood still, including Lily and Tom. They stared in horror at the partially-demolished hut and dangling, broken barrier arm, too stunned to move. Then, as if of one mind, they leaped into action.

'We'd better help,' Lily said urgently.

Their footsteps pounded on the stairs as they raced down, Lily close on Tom's heels, both of them practically swinging off the handrails as they rounded corners. They dashed across the carpark, Tom arriving at the hut first.

A dazed-looking lorry driver was emerging from the cab of his vehicle. The lorry, unlike the hut, appeared unscathed.

'You OK?' Tom asked the driver perfunctorily as he passed.

The man rubbed his neck.

'Yeah. Touch of whiplash, I think.' His mouth twisted. 'Don't know about the poor bloke in the hut, though.'

'You stay there, Lily,' Tom barked.

Seconds later, though, Tom emerged, dragging an apparently uninjured Sidney Lambert by the arm. Sidney in turn was dragging a bulging sack. Lily was willing to bet that sack contained pound coins.

'Oh, thank goodness for that,' Lily breathed, taking in the sight. 'I'll call the police,' she called across to Tom.

At the mention of the word, police, Sidney looked alarmed.

'Here, there's no need for that . . .'

Lily got out her mobile phone, rapidly

dialling 999.

'Someone will be with you in a couple of minutes,' the woman on the other end assured her.

'You can let go of me. I'm OK now,' Sidney grunted to Tom, attempting to pull his arm free.

'Not just yet, I don't think,' Tom said firmly, holding fast as Sidney tussled with him.

As Lily returned her phone to her pocket, the theme from *Doctor Zhivago* suddenly cut into the air, warblingly, discordantly played, as only an ice-ceam van could play it.

Looking up, her suspicions were confirmed. The bright yellow van parked loopsidedly and the middle-aged driver jumped out, rushing over to Sidney.

'Get out of here, Bert!' Sidney yelled, as Tom held him. 'They've called the cops!'

A look of terror passed through Bert's blue eyes, and he made a dash back to the ice-cream van. Lily sprang into action, racing over to the van and cutting Bert off before he could get there. Sirens could be heard in the air now, and Bert turned, making for the exit. Lily ran after him.

'Be careful, Lily!' Tom shouted.

Their footsteps pounded down the street of narrow Victorian houses. Bert took a side turning down an alley and Lily pursued him. Fortunately for Lily, the alley was a dead end, and she cornered him.

She grabbed the man's checked sleeve. For good measure, Lily tried to remember the words she'd heard so often on television.

'You do not have to say anything,' she panted, 'but anything you do say may be used in evidence . . .'

Bert looked at her as if she was mad.

'What the heck are you doing, lady? I'm an ice-cream man.'

'I'm making a citizen's arrest,' Lily said.

The man gave her a scornful once-over.

'Oh, yeah? You and whose army?'

Rapid footsteps sounded down the alley as Tom and Jamie appeared, both dishevelled from running.

'You were saying?' Tom asked Bert pointedly.

Bert subsided into sullen silence.

'Jamie!' Lily exclaimed, looking at him with pleased surprise. 'How did you get here?'

Jamie shrugged his well-muscled shoulders, every inch the knight in shining armour if only he didn't have that strange, unreadable look on his face.

'Tom called me on my mobile. Said my assistance might be required.'

'Certainly did,' Tom added drily. 'A bit more haste and less speed might have been in order. I told you to look after that car!' he added pointedly.

'Sorry, boss,' Jamie muttered. Lily was about to ask what on earth they were arguing about, when Bert distracted her.

'You might as well come quietly,' Tom said, grabbing Bert's other arm, while Jamie came to assist Lily. 'The police have taken charge now, and they've arrested your mate, Sidney.'

CHAPTER EIGHT

Bert allowed them to escort him back to the carpark, muttering all the while about ringing his solicitor.

'Good grief!' Lily exclaimed suddenly, when a policeman had relieved them of Bert. Her eyes were transfixed to a point across the carpark. 'What happened to the Range Rover, Jamie?'

The gleaming, metallic green vehicle stood discarded by the barrier at the carpark's entrance, its bonnet crumpled into the barrier's concrete base. It looked strangely like it had melted in the sun.

Jamie flicked a glance at Tom, saying again, 'I'm sorry, Tom.' Tom said nothing, but got his mobile phone out of his pocket and keyed in a number.

'How did it happen?' Lily asked Jamie, eyes wide, while police activity bustled around them.

Jamie looked guilty, and distinctly uneasy.

'As I was driving in, top speed, the barrier arm was dangling, half-broken. It started to fall, and I swerved to avoid it. Unfortunately though, in doing so I crashed into the concrete base.'

'Still, you're OK, that's the main thing,' Lily said, reaching across to pat Jamie on the arm.

Tom didn't look quite so sympathetic. He glanced across, while busy speaking into his mobile.

'Yes, that's right, Colin,' he was saying into the phone. 'Yes, I'm afraid it looks like a write-off.' He held the phone slightly away from his ear so that Lily and Jamie could hear the verbal torrent on the other end.

Feeling a pang of sympathy for Jamie, Lily looked across to meet his eyes.

'He's gone! Jamie's gone!' she exclaimed, gazing across the carpark.

'Strange,' Tom murmured, looking up. 'Look, Colin,' he went on, into the phone, 'Jamie seems to have done a vanishing act. I'm really sorry about what happened, and I'll ring you later.'

There was a commotion of activity across the carpark. Lily sighed, feeling as if she had had enough excitement to last her a lifetime.

'Looks like we might as well head back to Brighton as soon as possiblc,' she said as they watched Sidney Lambert and Bert Wilkinson being bundled into the back of a police car. 'I'm not going to hide from the likes of Gerry Lambert for ever.'

Tom agreed saying, 'The police are bound to want to take statements from us. Jamie included.' His brow furrowed. 'God only knows where he's got to.' He glanced around him again. 'We ought to hand over our file to the police, too, containing all the evidence we've collected on the counterfeiting activities in this part of the south.'

'Good thinking,' Lily commended him. 'Well, it looks like we've nailed Sidney Lambert comprehensively. That's two more pieces of lowlife scum off the streets, who hopefully won't be conning any innocent people for a while.' Her eyes narrowed. 'Shame we couldn't catch big brother, Gerry, so decisively in the act!'

'Mmm,' Tom murmured, his eyes meeting hers. 'One senses that Gerry Lambert is the real big fish here.' He clamped his mouth shut abruptly as a middle-aged policeman approached them.

'Sir, madam,' the policeman said, 'if you wouldn't mind following us to the station, we'd like to take a statement from both of you.'

Lily and Tom were sitting on regulation plastic seats in the police station, waiting to be called to make their statements, when Lily's mobile phone bleeped. There was a text message which she read, wide-eyed, before passing the phone to Tom.

'*Having celebratory drink at Coach and Horses,*' Tom read, under his breath. '*Meet me there when U R ready.* Wasn't that the pub near the carpark?' Tom added.

'So that's where Jamie got to,' Lily muttered bemusedly, slipping the phone back into her bag. 'I wonder why he was so desperate for a drink?'

'Hmm,' Tom agreed, leaning confidentially close to Lily in a way that made her skin tingle. 'Call me uncharitable, Lil, but I can't help wondering if it was because our Jamie didn't want to talk to the police.'

Two hours later, their statements made, Tom drove Lily back over to the east of the town. The sun was just starting to sink lower in the sky.

'Turns out the local police had been after Sidney and his pals for ages. The lorry crashing into the hut brought things to a head but the sergeant was pleased when I handed over our file. Said there should be enough information there for them to nail them,' Tom said.

They drove past Sidney's carpark, deserted now, and parked his car in the street outside the Coach and Horses. As he and Lily emerged from the car, Tom glanced warily down the street.

'I must be mad, leaving my precious car unattended in an area like this.'

'Oh, don't worry,' Lily said with brisk assurance. 'You've set the engine immobiliser, Tom. It'll be fine.' She frowned bemusedly. 'I'm more concerned about whether Jamie will still be in there after all this time or whether he'll have disappeared again, goodness knows where.'

'Yes,' Tom added, his wide mouth twisting.

'I for one would really like to have a word with my good friend, James.'

Jamie was propping up the bar in the small, old-fashioned pub, looking slightly the worse for wear, and chatting to a couple of regulars. Despite the fact that it was not quite six o'clock, the pub was surprisingly busy.

'Lily! Tom!' Jamie greeted them warmly. 'I thought you were never coming! What'll it be? No, don't tell me, Lily, a dry white wine spritzer. Although, to be honest,' he added, in a theatrical aside, 'this doesn't look much like your dry white wine kind of establishment.'

'Yes, well, I don't normally drink at this time of day. But as we're, um, celebrating, any kind of white wine will be lovely, thank you, Jamie,' Lily murmured, trying not to meet the eye of the barman.

'You'd better make mine a lemonade,' Tom added gruffly, 'seeing as I'm driving.'

Carrying their drinks, they all trooped over to an unoccupied table near a small, grimy window.

'So, what was the disappearing act all about, Jamie?' Lily asked innocently, sipping her wine.

'What? Oh, I was just taken over by a sudden, raging thirst.' He winked at her.

Tom cleared his throat and said, 'Anyway, here's to catching our man. Or rather, men,' he said, lifting his glass.

'Ssh!' Jamie muttered, looking wary. 'Half

102

their cronies are probably in here.' Sure enough, a heavily made-up woman sitting at the bar glanced over at them. Looking resentful, Jamie chinked his glass against Tom's and Lily's.

'Well,' Tom hissed, his eyes flashing tawny sparks, 'wasn't this pub a rather poor choice as a venue for celebrating their arrests, then?'

'I don't know why you had to shop those two blokes to the police, anyway, Tom,' Jamie muttered. 'Couldn't you have just got the info you needed to write your article and been done with it?'

'But, Jamie,' Lily interrupted, trying to stay reasonable, 'the whole point was to stop men like them ruining small businesses belonging to people like my father! You knew that when you agreed to get involved with this.'

Jamie hissed, leering across the table towards them, saying, 'But don't you see, thanks to you two, Gerry Lambert will probably be on to us now? And he's not the sort of man you want to mess with.'

There was a look of desperation in his pale blue eyes that got Lily wondering exactly what was going on in Jamie's life.

'Come on, you two!' Lily exclaimed, glancing from one man to the other. 'Let's not fight. We're supposed to be celebrating a job well done.'

'Truce,' Tom muttered reluctantly.

'Truce,' Jamie agreed, picking up his whisky

103

glass and downing the remainder. 'Aah. I could do with another one of those. Tom, mate, you couldn't, could you?' He pulled out the linings of his trouser pockets. 'The thing is, I seem to have run out of money.'

Tom scraped back his chair.

'It's OK, Jamie. It was my round anyway.' He eyed Jamie's dishevelled figure.

As Tom disappeared to the bar, Jamie said, 'Excuse me, Lily, I must nip to the toilet.'

Left alone, Lily's eyes were drawn towards Tom's tall, jeans-clad figure at the bar. As he waited for the drinks, one of the locals had approached him, the heavily made-up woman in her fifties who'd been watching them earlier. Despite her age and the heavy hand with which her make-up had been applied, Lily felt a sudden, inexplicable pang of jealousy towards her as she leaned closer to Tom, laughing at a shared joke.

It was obvious she had been attracted by Tom's undeniable good looks. The woman had clearly once been stunningly attractive herself, with her vibrant red hair, now obviously out of a bottle, pretty face and curvaceous figure, clad in a lacy white blouse and short skirt. Tom bought the woman a drink, treating her to his slow, lazy grin before picking up his drinks and departing back to the table.

Lily blurted out the words before she could restrain herself.

104

'I never knew you had a thing for older women.'

Passing her her drink, Tom turned to look at Lily in surprise.

'Surely you're not jealous of Belle, are you?'

'Belle!' Lily spluttered, gazing across at the woman who had returned to her port and lemon, and her cigarette. 'Well, I might have guessed.'

Tom leaned closer to Lily, lowering his voice. She saw that his eyes were alight with a familiar look.

'As a matter of fact, Lily, once we got chatting, Belle was telling me something extremely interesting. I might need to have another little chat with her later.' He glanced at the bustling pub around him which seemed to have got even busier. 'I can't really explain now, Lily. It'll have to wait for later. Where's Jamie?' Tom added, changing the subject.

Lily suppressed her jealousy, saying, 'The gents.' She glanced at her watch. 'He's been ages.'

At that moment a door banged across the small pub and Jamie reappeared, tottering slightly.

'Are you OK?' Lily asked anxiously, as he sat back down at their table, looking pale and washed out, his dark hair splashed with water.

'Yes, thanks, Lily. I feel better now, anyway, if you see what I mean.'

Lily didn't ask him to elucidate. Jamie glanced at the whisky Tom had ordered him.

'Maybe some of that black coffee would be in order now,' Tom put in grimly. 'I noticed a percolator behind the bar.'

'I'll get it,' Lily said quickly, rising to her feet.

'A black coffee, please,' she asked the barman.

'Excuse me, love,' a sudden voice at her elbow said. Spinning round, Lily saw that it was Tom's older woman, Belle. 'I believe I was chatting to your boyfriend just now.' She glanced longingly over in Tom's direction.

'But he's not . . .' Lily broke in.

The woman interrupted her, 'If I was you, love, I wouldn't let a good-looking man like that slip through my fingers. Though you've got two lookers to choose from there.' She took a drag on her cigarette, regarding Lily through green eyes heavy with mascara, the lashes like spiders' legs. 'I was pretty like you once. Men flock to you, don't they?' She blew out a smoke ring, her expression growing bitter. 'Fat lot of good it does you in the end, though.'

'Oh, really?' Lily said politely.

Belle cackled, taking a swig of her drink.

'As I was telling your dishy boyfriend just now, I got involved with gangsters, didn't I, love? I became what you'd call a gangster's moll. That was my big mistake.'

106

'Gangsters?' Lily whispered, starting to realise why Tom had been so interested now.

Belle went on, taking another sip of her drink, 'I used to live in Brighton, you see, and about five years ago, I got into a relationship with a man called Gerry Lambert.'

Lily's blue eyes widened but she was careful not to reveal her excitement. Instead, she slipped unobtrusively on to the bar stool next to Belle.

'So you got on well with him, did you, this, er, Gerry?'

'He's a famous gangster, love. But maybe a nice girl like you wouldn't have heard of him. And, no, I didn't get on with Gerry particularly well, after the initial honeymoon period of our relationship.' Her eyes darkened. 'It didn't take me long to realise I was just one of his women. But something good did come out of that relationship.

'You see, one weekend, Gerry's brother, Sidney, came up to Brighton on a visit from Bournemouth. We were all down at Gerry's pub, the Beachcomber, on the Friday night, the whole gang, and, although Sidney was married, he and I hit it off right away.'

'Go on,' Lily said, enthralled, trying to imagine the stocky, tattooed Sidney as an object of passion.

'Well, it wasn't long before Sidney and I were having a love affair, but it was more than that, we had feelings for each other, too, and I

107

moved down here to Bournemouth to be with him.'

Belle looked Lily straight in the eye.

'The thing was, Gerry wasn't too keen on the fact that I'd ditched him for his little brother. So he told Sidney to dump me, stick with his wife.' Belle's eyes glittered like emeralds. 'And he did. So you see,' Belle went on bitterly, lifting her glass again, 'I've grown to hate them both, Gerry for ruining my life and Sidney for turning out to be weak.'

'That's a sad story, you poor thing.' Lily breathed sympathetically, seeing for the first time the pathos behind the woman's painted façade. 'I suppose, knowing both brothers intimately, you knew all their secrets.'

Belle threw back her head and laughed, that now-familiar cackle.

'If I didn't know better, love, I'd say you were fishing for information.' She leaned in. 'I'll come clean with you, love. I'm not stupid and news travels on the grapevine. I heard the police picked up Sidney this afternoon for the counterfeit scam, and Bert Wilkinson, too.' A spark of malicious enjoyment entered her eyes. 'I'm not going to lose any sleep over that.' She went on, 'I know you guys aren't from round here and I also overheard Gerry Lambert's name being mentioned at your table earlier. Let's say I put two and two together and made four.'

'I beg your pardon?' Lily asked, baffled.

'Come on, admit it, love. You're undercover police officers, aren't you?'

Lily blushed. 'Well, no. Tom's an investigative journalist, though, and we are working in conjunction with the police. Was there something you wanted to tell me?'

Belle's crimson lips blew another smoke ring.

'If the money's right, love.'

Lily's eyes widened.

'The money?' She tried to visualise the contents of her purse. 'I've only got about a hundred pounds on me and that's holiday spending money, you know.'

Belle raised a sculpted dark eyebrow.

'What about your friend, the investigative journalist?'

'I'll go and ask him,' Lily said quickly, sensing she was on to a winner. 'Stay right there.' She scuttled back to the bar table where Tom and Jamie were deep in conversation. The mood didn't seem too convivial, either.

'Tom,' Lily hissed, 'Belle's prepared to talk but she wants money.'

'I thought so, too,' Tom replied with a faint grin that creased the lines around his eyes.

He got out his wallet under the table, peeling off ten fifty-pound notes. Lily took the money and sped back to Belle.

'I'm scared, you see,' Belle admitted, tucking the notes into her handbag. 'I know too much about those Lambert boys. I'd be happier if they were both behind bars.'

She picked up a beer mat and began to write on the back with a pen from her handbag.

'What I've got to give you, love, is an address. But it's not just any old address.'

When Lily returned to the table, the beer mat tucked safely into her handbag, Tom and Jamie appeared to be in the middle of a heated discussion, oblivious to her presence.

'I still maintain that you shouldn't have brought the police into this,' Jamie was saying sulkily.

'Like I said before,' Tom replied in a low voice, 'Lily only agreed to get involved if part of the remit was to try to bring the criminals to justice.'

'Yes,' Jamie retorted. 'Well, maybe you should never have got Lily involved.' He snorted derisively. 'Heck, you probably only wanted her to come in on it because you fancied her.'

Lily burst out indignantly, 'Hey, please give me credit for having a mind of my own.' Both men spun round, noticing her presence for the first time.

Tom's eyes alighted on her face.

'Lily! You're back. Did you get what you wanted?'

'I certainly did.'

'Great. Well, let's get out of here. Coming,

Jamie?' Tom sounded as if he didn't much mind either way.

'Yes, boss,' Jamie muttered sarcastically.

The heavy pub door banged shut behind them. When the three of them were back out in the street, Lily took a lungful of clean air. She was about to tell Tom about her conversation with Belle when Jamie, still clearly under the influence of the alcohol he'd consumed, confronted Tom on the pavement.

Jamie pulled Tom's sleeve, tugging him round to face him.

'Come on, Tom, you still haven't answered my question. Did you only get Lily involved in all this because you fancied her?'

Tom squared up to him, slightly taller than the other man.

'Of course not! I felt that Lily had a valid personal contribution to make, because she's seen first-hand how counterfeiting can affect people's lives.'

Jamie sneered. 'So it was nothing to do with the fact that she's got blonde hair, blue eyes and legs that go on for ever?'

'Don't insult my intelligence, Jamie!' Lily put in angrily, sticking her head in between the two men.

'Anyway,' Tom went on, the expression in his eyes veiled, 'you couldn't exactly blame me if I was attracted to Lily, Jamie. After all, you've been chasing round after her like a lovesick puppy yourself.'

Jamie thrust his face closer to Tom's.

'Yes, and that's what you really can't stand, isn't it? The fact that Lily and I went out together, that she chose me over you. Why does that make you so angry, Tom?' Jamie's ice-blue eyes leered. 'Does it remind you unpleasantly of the time when your wife ran off with another man? Is that it?'

'Don't bring my ex-wife into this,' Tom said in a dangerously controlled voice, his eyes glittering with anger.

Lily was reminded with a jolt of how much Tom must still care for Tina.

'No, let's stick with the subject we were discussing,' Jamie said. 'Tom, I think you were a fool to get an ordinary, female member of the public involved in this.'

'Charming!' Lily burst out. 'Shall I just leave now?'

Tom turned to Lily and said, 'For your information, Lily, I don't for one minute regret asking you to become part of the investigation. I couldn't have done it without you.' He spun round to face Jamie, his supposed friend. 'Maybe I shouldn't have got you involved, Jamie. I know you've done some sterling work for us, and I'm very grateful for that, but your drinking and gambling have started to get out of hand again, and as for pranging my boss's car . . .'

'It was an accident!' Jamie bellowed. 'Give me a break, Tom. You're supposed to be

112

my friend.'

'Yes, well,' Tom said, some of his anger subsiding. 'One of the major elements of friendship is trust, Jamie. And, quite frankly, I don't feel I can trust you any more.'

'What do you mean?' Jamie asked, in a low, wary voice.

Tom looked awkward.

'Was it you who grassed on Lily and me to Gerry Lambert? Told him where we lived so that he could do our places over?'

There was a silence.

'No,' Jamie replied, bowing his dark, spiky head.

Lily noticed that Jamie was unable to meet their eyes.

'Jamie?' she pressed.

Finally Jamie looked up at her. His face was etched with misery.

'Oh, yes, all right then,' he muttered. 'I did tell Gerry Lambert about the two of you. Told him Tom was an investigative reporter and Lily was helping him, too. But only because his thugs threatened me!' Jamie blurted quickly.

'They threatened you?' Lily breathed. 'That time in the casino? That's terrible, Jamie.' Her eyes darkened. 'But you should have warned us afterwards!'

'I wanted to continue as if nothing was wrong,' Jamie said. 'I wanted to keep working for both of you.'

113

Tom was staring at Jamie.

'We told you all our secrets, Jamie,' he said slowly, an evening breeze blowing his hair. 'And all the time you were a viper in our midst.'

'I was scared,' Jamie admitted. 'I'm still scared. In fact,' he added, 'I don't think I'll go back to Brighton for a bit.'

'Maybe you and I had better keep out of each other's way, too, for a while, Jamie,' Tom said coldly. 'If our friendship is to stand any chance of surviving. In the meantime, thanks for what you've done for us.' He took out his wallet, peeled off a wodge of notes and handed them to Jamie. 'Here's your money.'

'You're paying me off,' Jamie said dully. 'My thirty pieces of silver.'

Looking at him, Lily wondered how she could ever have felt anything for Jamie. All she felt now was pity.

CHAPTER NINE

They left Jamie at the Coach and Horses. He had gone back in to enquire about accommodation in the area.

'See, you needn't have worried, Tom,' Lily murmured as they got back into the car. 'Your car's all in one piece.'

'Mmm. That worry seems rather insignificant now, doesn't it, after what happened with Jamie? It almost seems bad form to ask you what you found out from Belle.'

Lily got the beer mat out of her bag, flipping it over to show Tom the address on the back.

'It's the address of the old chap who prints the notes. It's on the outskirts of Brighton. He keeps the printer in his garage.'

At Lily's words, that familiar spark lit up Tom's eyes.

'Bingo, Lily! Now we can give the police everything they need to nail Gerry Lambert.' He leaned across to kiss her firmly on the lips. 'Well done. You did brilliantly.' Lily was surprised at how that brief, congratulatory kiss sent her pulse racing.

The following morning, Saturday, they checked out of the Hotel Sunshine and prepared to start the drive back to Brighton.

Lily sighed as the car approached the outskirts of Brighton, crawling along the seafront road, busy with weekend traffic. It was a cloudy day, and it looked as though it might rain.

'Penny for them?' Tom asked, taking his eyes briefly off the road to glance across at her.

Lily felt embarrassed.

'Oh, I was just thinking about returning to an empty flat, with the prospect of baked beans on toast for lunch.'

Tom concentrated on the road ahead.

'Is your father still at your brother's, then?'

'Yes. He's not due back till the middle of next week. I phoned him last night before I went to bed. They're all having a great time.' Lily laughed. 'I feel quite left out, actually.'

Tom negotiated a roundabout.

'Well, you could always take your life in your own hands and come to my place for a bite, before we go down to the police station to hand over the file on Gerry Lambert. Better still,' he went on, 'we could get a takeaway pizza or something for lunch. Then you wouldn't have to risk a trip to casualty with food poisoning,' he joked.

'I'm sure you're a fantastic cook,' Lily replied, laughing. She was touched by Tom's offer. 'If you're sure you don't mind, that

116

would be nice, anyway.' She frowned suddenly. 'Although maybe I ought to get home, check that Paul and Nathan haven't got any problems with the shop, and that Gerry Lambert hasn't been around, causing trouble.'

'Tell you what,' Tom said, changing gear. 'I'll wait for you outside while you drop off your bags and check that things are ticking over OK at the shop, if you like.'

Despite his casual tone, Lily was aware of how kind Tom was being.

'You don't have to do all that for me,' she said, blushing.

Tom flicked her a quick look, direct in the eye.

'I like to,' he said simply. His words, and his tone, sent Lily's mind spinning into confused pleasure.

*   *   *

Some time later, Lily flopped back on to Tom's sofa, replete.

'Mmm, that was delicious. Ham and pineapple's my all-time favourite.'

'Well, there's one more piece.' Tom grinned, waving the box at her. 'I'll fight you for it.'

'No, thanks, Tom.' Lily smiled back. 'That was lovely, but I couldn't eat another mouthful.' She dabbed at her mouth with one of the paper serviettes that had come with the pizza, loathe to think that she might be smiling idiotically at Tom with tomato sauce all over her face. At least they hadn't had garlic bread, so they wouldn't be breathing garlic every time they spoke to each other.

'Would you like anything else to drink?' Tom asked, interrupting her crazy thoughts. 'I can even run to a cup of tea.'

'Just another glass of water would be great. Thanks.'

As Tom disappeared from his sitting-room, Lily had another chance to study her surroundings. His first-floor apartment was lovely, part of a Regency house on the seafront, with high ceilings, original plaster mouldings and stunning views of the sea from the long sash windows. The décor was sympathetic, too—neutral and understated, accented by the odd antique of mellow, dark wood.

Tom returned, with two glasses of water on a tray. He handed Lily hers and, flopping down on the sofa next to her, took a long drink of his.

'Lovely place you've got here,' Lily commented. Inadvertently, her knee brushed Tom's denim-clad one, and she blushed, pulling it away.

'Yes,' Tom replied dryly. 'Thankfully Gerry Lambert and company didn't trash it for me while I was away.' He paused. 'So, everything had been running smoothly at the shop in your absence?'

Lily nodded, her hair slipping over her shoulders.

'Paul and Nathan thought there had been a slight upturn in business, and that maybe Mason's has turned a corner. Those two are probably more competent than I am, really. They've been doing it for longer, after all.'

The corners of her mouth curled.

'Are you still itching to get back to your real job?' Tom asked.

'Oh, yes,' Lily replied eagerly, flicking back her hair. 'I'm due to go back the Monday after next, and I can't wait. I think the time's right, too. Dad seems to be doing really well now.' She reached over to touch the coffee table. 'Touch wood, and what with the business starting to do better, too. The only thing now will be for me to find a place of my own.'

'Well, I'm glad things are going better for Eddie.' Tom paused, clearing his throat. 'Lily,' he asked suddenly, checking his watch, 'I know we really ought to be getting down to the police station soon but, first, could we talk about us?'

'About us?' Lily asked, surprised. 'There's nothing really to say, is there?' she said quickly. 'I mean, I know we've kissed a couple of times, but don't worry, I know it didn't mean anything. After all,' she added, meeting his eyes with difficulty, so close to hers, 'you've only recently split up from your wife, and I know your feelings are still a bit raw about all that.'

'What do you mean, Lily? I told you I was over all that, didn't I?'

'I know,' Lily said, chewing her lip, 'but it must have been so awful, to have your wife suddenly leave you for someone else, when you'd thought you were both perfectly happy.'

'Lily,' Tom said bluntly, 'I've got something to tell you. By the time Tina was having her affair with David, I was no longer in love with her anyway. Things between us had already deteriorated beyond repair.'

Lily felt a small glimmer of hope in her heart. 'Really?'

'What about you, though?' Tom was going on. 'You've recently come out of a long-term relationship, too. And then there was Jamie.'

'As for Ryan,' Lily said firmly, 'I've realised that I'm well and truly over him, the rat. As for Jamie, I tried to tell you before, that although I liked him, I realised he and I weren't really compatible.'

A smile spread slowly across Tom's face as he said, 'Do you know what, though? Jamie was right about one thing.'

'What's that?' Lily breathed, enthralled.

'Because I'd already seen my wife run off with a friend of mine, that was why I couldn't stand to see you stolen out from under my nose, by Jamie.' Tom lifted a hand to cup her cheek. 'Because I've really grown to like you, Lily.'

Gently, he drew her face towards his, and kissed her. Lily responded passionately, twining her hands behind his neck and pulling him closer. So what if Tom was allergic to commitment? In the height of her passion, Lily recklessly felt she would take whatever scraps of relationship he was prepared to throw her.

When they pulled apart breathlessly, Tom looked intently at her, a strange smile playing at the corners of his mouth.

'I've been wanting to do that for a long time. The thing is, Lily, I . . .'

At that moment there was a loud crash from outside the room. Lily and Tom sprang apart, Lily's heart pounding for a different reason now.

Seconds later the door to the room burst open, and in came a stocky, suit-clad man, with a shaven head. After him, resplendent in a sheepskin coat despite the mild weather, strode Gerry Lambert. Lily's heart contracted in fear.

Tom leaped to his feet. Lily stood, too.

'What the heck's going on here, Lambert?'

Gerry Lambert did not answer the question.

'So you're back, I see,' he growled, looking from Tom to Lily. His cold blue eyes glittered menacingly.

Tom said, moving threateningly towards

Gerry, 'I don't remember inviting you to enter my home, let alone smash your way in.'

The other thug, who had followed Gerry Lambert in, came and placed himself between his master and Tom. Ignoring the comment, Gerry went and made himself comfortable on the sofa. He looked from Tom to Lily again, in a way that made Lily squirm.

'So, what do you two know about my brother being arrested?'

'No comment,' Lily said quickly, before Tom could say something more inflammatory.

Gerry looked at her.

'The thing is, you two shouldn't keep sticking your noses into other people's business. You might suddenly find you're in too deep.'

He was right, Lily thought. I'm in way too deep.

'Anyway,' Gerry went on, 'where's your pal, Jimmy Donovan, if that's his real name? Only, I've got some unfinished business to settle with him.'

'Jimmy is no longer my responsibility,' Tom replied coolly.

Gerry rested his arms along the back of the sofa.

'Whatever. I'll sort him out later. With regard to the two of you, though, I can tell you both that I've got no intention of meeting the same fate as poor old Sidney.' He shook his head, tutting regretfully. 'My baby brother never did have quite what it took.'

Tom came and stood over Gerry Lambert. Lily saw anger flash through Tom's tawny eyes.

'Sorry to disappoint you, Gerry, but after we've shown the police what we've got on you, they'll have no choice but to lock you up and throw away the key.'

Lambert sat bolt upright on the sofa, his face suspicious.

'What is it, McCleod? What've you got on me?' He laughed dryly. 'Besides a few photos and fake notes?'

'If only you knew,' Lily murmured, half to herself, thinking of the counterfeiter's address.

Lambert's eyes swivelled to her, and Lily wished she had kept her mouth shut. The man made an obvious effort to calm himself. That charm, as fake as his notes, settled over his persona.

'Anyway, Miss Mason, Mr McCleod, do sit down. Let's have a civil chat.'

He indicated the two armchairs either side of him.

Lily sat. Tom sighed. 'Well, seeing as it looks like we're going to be here for some time.' He sat.

Gerry smiled pleasantly.

'So where's the stuff you've got on me? I'd appreciate it if you'd tell me, or my two friends here, Robert and Crusher . . .' He gestured towards the two shaven thugs. '. . . will be obliged to smash up this nice place.'

'Don't look at me,' Lily muttered, her heart pounding uncontrollably in her chest. She glanced at Tom, wondering how he intended to play this. 'It isn't my flat after all.'

'Oh, shame,' Gerry said. 'And I thought you two were such a cosy pair of lovebirds.'

Remembering their recent, passionate kiss, Lily flushed.

'Maybe you shouldn't make assumptions about people you don't know, Mr Lambert,' she said coolly.

Lambert smiled, revealing a glinting gold tooth.

'Ah, a lady with spirit. My favourite.'

Growing impatient, the blond, shaven one, Robert, moved threateningly towards Tom.

'Come on, where's the stuff?'

'The stuff?' Tom glanced warily at Lambert's henchman. 'Oh, very well,' he muttered grudgingly. 'It's in that desk over there.' Tom gestured carelessly towards the bureau on the right hand side of the room.

Lily glanced at Tom, surprised and a little disappointed at this easy capitulation.

The two henchmen rushed over to the desk and began flinging the contents of drawers haphazardly on to the carpet. There were papers, books, folders. They flicked through them, only to cast them away in disgust.

Lily winced at the chaos, though Tom appeared unperturbed. When the desk was nearly emptied, Tom scratched his chin idly.

'Or maybe I moved it,' he mused.

Anger flared in Lambert's cold eyes.

'If you're playing games with me, McCleod . . .' He smacked his hand on the coffee table, jolting Lily's glass of water.

The darker one, Crusher, was beside Tom in an instant. He grabbed his collar, fist curled threateningly towards Tom's face. Lily emitted a low gasp of dismay.

'Oh, dear,' Lambert said. 'Looks like you're making Crusher angry.'

Tom shook himself angrily free of Crusher's grasp, straightening his shirt collar with typical vanity.

'On second thoughts,' he said casually, 'maybe I put it in the cupboard over there.' Tom indicated the antique mahogany sideboard on the other side of the room.

'Sure?' Crusher snarled mockingly.

'Sure,' Tom replied blandly, meeting the man's gaze.

'No more time wasting, please,' Gerry said. He glanced at Lily. 'It would be such a shame to have to mar this young lady's beauty.'

'You wouldn't dare touch me, you, you creep!' Lily burst out, anger overcoming her fear.

'Wouldn't I?'

'Just leave her out of this,' Tom said in a

tone of barely-controlled fury.

He moved to get out of his chair but Lily flashed him a warning glance, and he sat back down.

'Well, don't just stand there,' Gerry snapped at Crusher. 'Try the sideboard!'

'Nothing here,' the blond-stubbled thug muttered several minutes later.

He picked up a carriage clock from the top of the sideboard and dropped it carelessly to the floor.

'Hey, watch it,' Tom growled, getting to his feet.

Crusher, with blank, wintry grey eyes, moved across to Lily. He took a pair of secateurs out of his suit-jacket pocket, and a pencil from the other side. He snipped the pencil smartly in half with the secateurs, then picked up Lily's hand by the little finger. Terrified, Lily submitted.

'He's very good at pruning, is our Crusher,' Gerry smirked. 'Big fan of Alan Titchmarsh.'

Tom was across the room in a shot, shoving Crusher out of the way.

'If you're going to cut anyone's finger off, you brainless idiot, it'll be mine.'

Crusher raised the secateurs towards Tom.

'No, Tom!' Lily screamed. 'Just tell them where the stuff is!'

There was a scuffle at the door, and suddenly two more men had entered the room.

126

The first, a thick-set, assured-looking man in middle-age, flipped open an identity card.

'Detective Sergeant Jack Thomson, Brighton CID.' He paused, looking around the disordered room, at the frozen tableau of people. 'What's going on here, then?'

Gerry Lambert turned on his charming smile.

'Just having a friendly chat with my pals here, officer.'

The chain of events had left Lily feeling shell-shocked and bemused.

'Wh-what are you doing here, Detective Sergeant?' she asked the policeman in amazement. 'I mean, we're very glad you're here, but how . . . ?'

'Phone call from a Mr Colin Bruce of the Brighton Clarion. Said some suspicious characters had been sniffing around his offices this morning, and he had a sneaking suspicion his colleague, Tom McCleod, was heading for trouble, that he was in deeper than he was letting on.'

'Colin,' Tom said, with the hint of a grin. 'I might have known. Good old Col, always did have a nose for the truth.'

D S Thomson moved forward to Gerry Lambert.

'I'm arresting you for causing criminal damage. You do not have to say anything but anything you do say may be given in evidence. You do not have to mention when questioned something which you later rely on in court.'

'Criminal damage?' Lambert echoed mockingly.

'Yes, that'll do for starters,' the other policeman said. 'A smashed front door.'

Tom went over to the coffee table and produced a box file from the ledge underneath it where, Lily realised to her surprise, it had been all along.

'And when you've finished on the criminal damage, I think you'll find, D S Thomson, that there's plenty here for you to get your teeth into. There's an address written on the back of a beer mat which might be of particular interest.'

Lily gazed at Tom in admiration—and recently-discovered love.

*　　　*　　　*

The police phoned for their contract repair man instantly, who came and patched up Tom's door within the space of half an hour. By then, the policemen had long since bundled away Gerry Lambert and his thugs and Lily and Tom were on their own in the flat once again.

'That's that then,' Tom said, flopping down, exhausted. 'Hopefully my article will go down a storm. Colin told me on the phone this morning that the editor of one of the big tabloids has already got wind of it, and been on the phone to him.' Tom's mouth twisted. 'Now all I've got to do is put the thing together.'

'Piece of cake,' Lily teased, from beside him on the sofa. 'And I'll go back to being a database administrator next week. Thank goodness. I'll start looking at flats, too.'

Tom sighed and said, 'Well, at least all those guests dropping in like that saved us a trip to the station to deliver our evidence.'

'Not really.' Lily grinned back. 'Seeing as we've still got to go to the station in a second to make our statements.'

'That can wait a couple of minutes,' Tom said firmly, laying an arm along the back of the sofa, gently caressing Lily's hair. A half-smile played on his mouth. 'Now, where were we, when we were so rudely interrupted?'

So he just wanted to kiss her again!

'Really, Tom, pleasant though it was, I hardly think now's the time.'

'I didn't mean the kiss, you fool,' Tom interrupted with a frustrated growl. His hair flopped in his face and he shoved it impatiently aside. 'Much though I'd like to repeat the experience.'

Lily shivered with anticipated pleasure.

'No,' Tom said and frowned, 'I have the feeling I was about to say something important, Lily, regarding my feelings towards you.'

Here it comes, the big brush-off.

'I know we're attracted to each other, but I also know you're wary of commitment,' Lily said calmly, 'and that, despite your protestations to the contrary, I think maybe you're still carrying feelings towards your ex-wife.' She shrugged. 'It's understandable.'

'Didn't you listen to any of what I told you?' Tom asked impatiently, his face disarmingly near to hers. There was a rare flash of emotion in his eyes. 'My feelings for my ex-wife died long ago. It's you I care about, Lily, you're the one who, despite everything, I appear to have fallen in love with. Well, are you going to say something?' Tom demanded, looking uncharacteristically disquieted. 'Is there any chance that you feel the same way?'

Lily's heart leaped ecstatically.

'Oh, Tom,' she burst out, her habitual calm broken. 'Of course I love you, though I may have attempted to convince myself otherwise.'

'Say it again,' Tom commanded, still looking unconvinced.

'What?'

'You know.'

Lily grinned.

'I love you, Tom. Hadn't you guessed? Or has your journalistic instinct let you down this time?'

She fell into his arms, which seemed the most natural thing in the world, and they kissed for a long time. When they pulled apart Lily gazed disbelievingly up at him.

'It's OK,' she murmured. 'I won't demand anything of you. I know you're allergic to marriage, after what's happened.'

'I never said anything of the sort.' Tom pulled back to gaze tenderly down at her. 'I've got nothing against marriage, if it's to the right person. And I think I may have found the right person this time.'

'Hmm, my dad would be pleased. He likes you. Still, maybe we should start with a date first,' Lily murmured.

Suddenly she sat up straighter, glancing at her watch.

'In fact, haven't we got a date right now, with Detective Sergeant Thomson, down at the station?'

'D S Thomson can wait a couple of minutes more,' Tom said, leaning forward to kiss her tenderly once again.